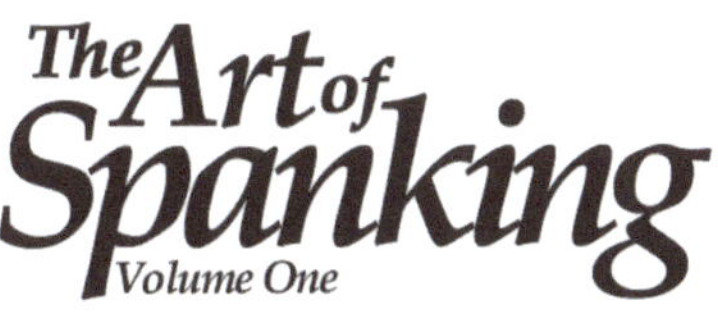

Pictorial erotica for the spanking connoisseur

Dedicated to all the beautiful talent photographed herein

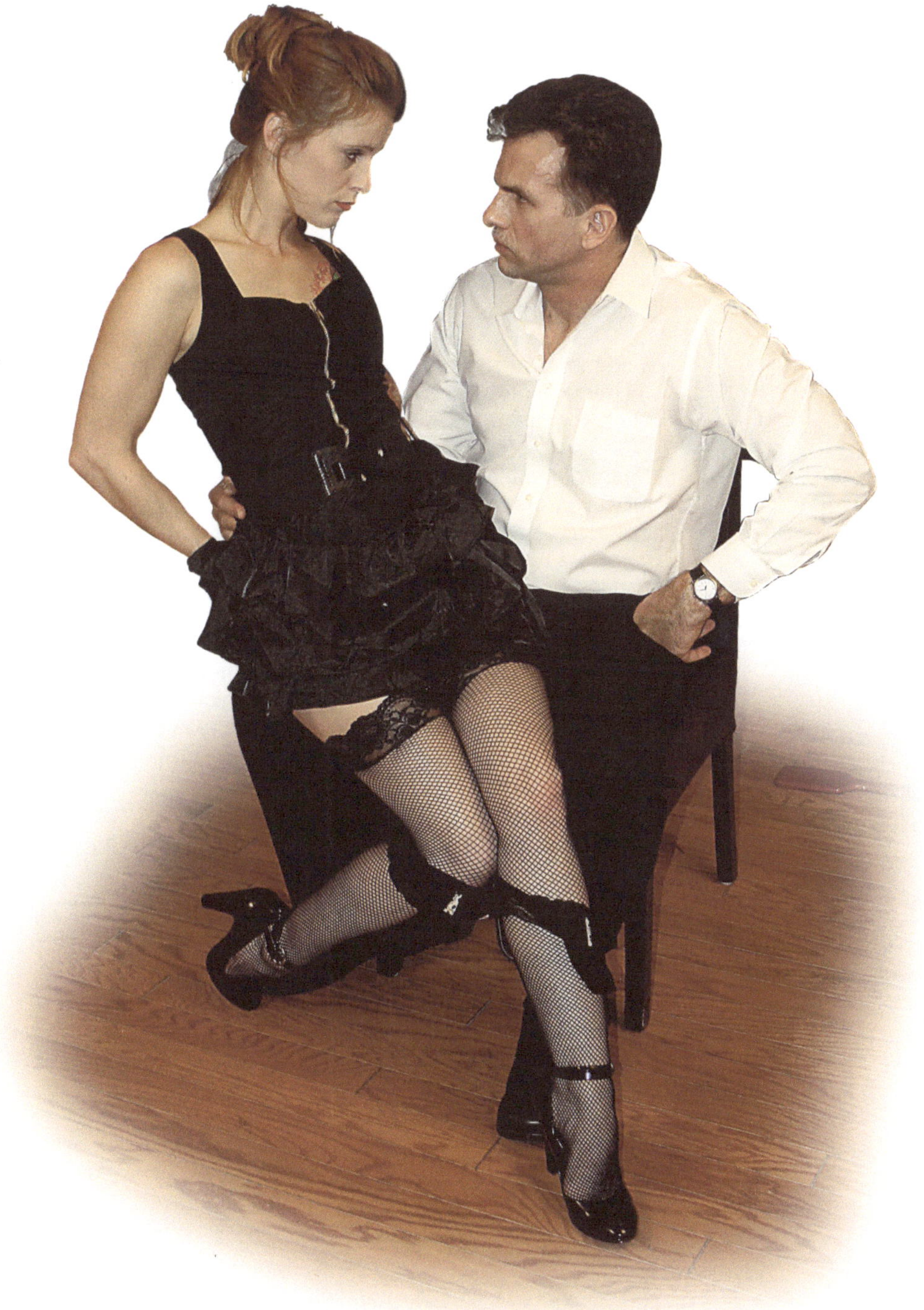

On our front cover Samantha Woodley and Arthur Sire
On our back cover and left, Nikki Rouge and Steve Fuller

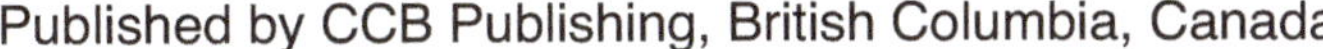
Published by CCB Publishing, British Columbia, Canada

Shadow Lane's **The Art of Spanking Volume One**
Editor **Eve Howard**
Art Director **Butch Simms**
Photography by **Butch Simms** and **Tony Elka**
Illustrations by **Brian Tarsis**
visit us @ www.shadowlane.com

Shadow Lane's The Art of Spanking Volume One:
Pictorial erotica for the spanking connoisseur

ISBN-13 978-1-926918-00-6
First Edition

Library and Archives Canada Cataloguing in Publication
Howard, Eve, 1953-
Shadow Lane's the art of spanking : pictorial erotica for the spanking connoisseur / edited by Eve Howard. —1st ed.
ISBN 978-1-926918-00-6 (v. 1)
Also available in electronic format.
1. Corporal punishment--Pictorial works.
2. Fetishism (Sexual behavior)--Pictorial works.
3. Photography, Erotic.
I. Title. II. Title: Art of spanking.
TR676.H69 2010 779'.28 C2010-905043-6

Publisher: CCB Publishing, British Columbia, Canada
www.ccbpublishing.com

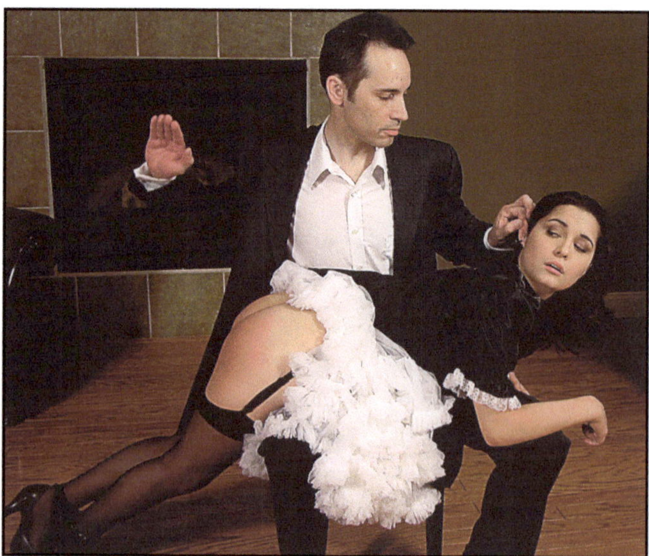

The Art of Spanking

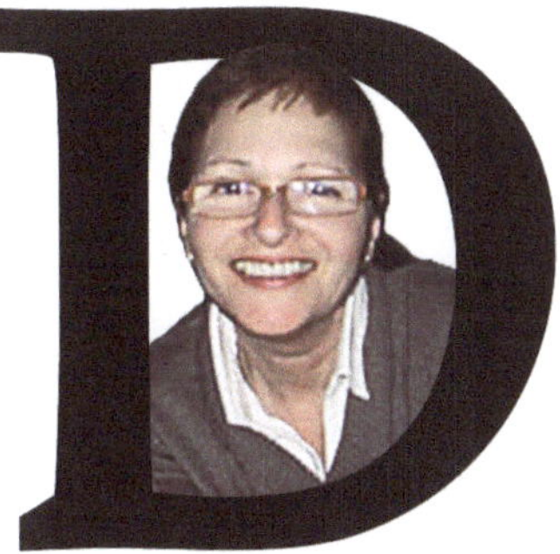

Dominance and submission. If you're into it you see it all around you, every day. Ad men, television writers, comedians, artists, even musicians and filmmakers grab a little of it here and there and fold it into their spin. It's very seductive. Sometimes it even endows the universe with a brand new fetishist. In the 50's it happened so innocently, while reading a comic book or watching Superman on TV. Lois and Jimmy got tied up together every episode, helpless and against their will, wriggling back to back, she in white gloves, he in a bow tie. In the comic book, Superman spanked Lois, in her dream sequence. These images stuck with us, implanting their seeds of painful desire, or in some cases, just a desire for pain. The most exciting aspect of an action fetish like bondage or spanking, is control. Dominants exert control, submissives surrender it, what is interesting is how.

This is a book about the power of spanking, its beauty and charm. Because it is intended for the pleasure of spanking enthusiasts, it is filled with unveiled damsels in distress, displayed mostly over the knee. In a spanking journal such as this, the focus must ever be on the bare bottoms of alluring women. But as every true connoisseur knows, there is more to spanking than the color pink. The people you will meet in the pages of this book are real, with individualistic personalities to match their arresting faces and expressive attitudes. They didn't get into this book by accident. A persistent fascination with spanking, mingled with a compulsion to perform in and create spanking erotica brought them to our studio. You might call models super spankers, people who have to take their spanking interest one step further than playing, by exhibiting themselves to the world at large while engaged in this volatile and yet highly intimate activity.

Shadow Lane has published spanking magazines since the late 1980's, our most popular publication being Stand Corrected. But this is our first publication in ten years and the first Shadow Lane publication to be all color. We've divided this issue into themes of major interest to spanking fans, defined by our most provocative photos.

Some spanking people get ruffled when they are lumped in with the BDSM subculture. We all like the "discipline" part of BDSM, eventually try the bondage, roundly reject the concept of slave and master and admit to being only mildly sadomasochistic (if pressed). Most female spanking enthusiasts would sooner surrender control to a Mr. Knightly than a Marquis de Sade. The dominant should be strict, but also gentlemanly, and full of all the kindness and respect that term implies. The terms "sense and sensibility" might well have been invented to describe the qualities sought by thinking women who seek sexual fulfillment by ceding control to their lovers.

We spanking folk are fated to be misunderstood and misrepresented by sensationalists, who would characterize us as anything but the subtle and sophisticated adventurers that we are. But the more we connect with each other, the more parties we attend, the more we date, play, and fall in love in the scene, the more convinced we enthusiasts become of the fact that spanking well is the best revenge.

To find out more about Shadow Lane, visit our website www.shadowlane.com where you can shop securely for fine spanking erotica and participate in the spanking scene through our exclusive members' clubhouse and personal ads. Be proactive, post an ad, chat, come to our next party. After over twenty years in the scene we have learned that networking does pay off.

Best wishes,

Eve Howard

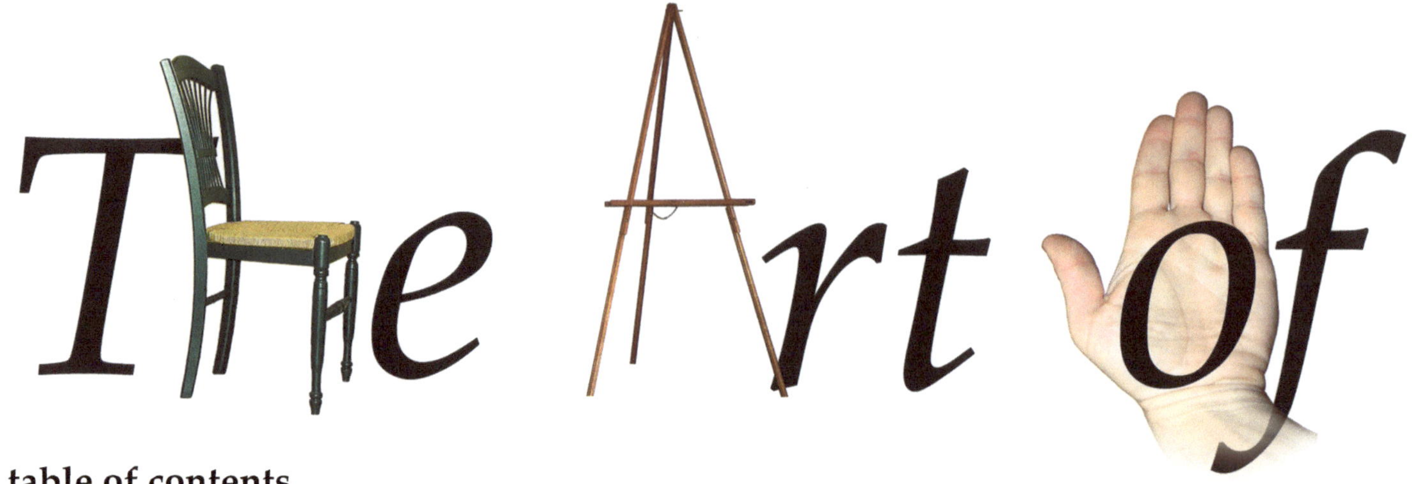

table of contents

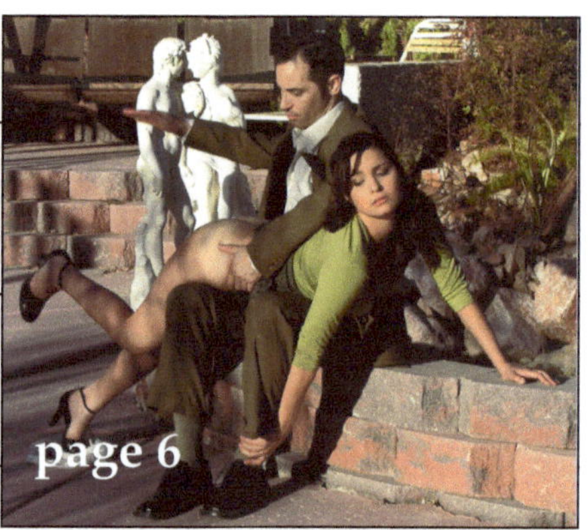
page 6

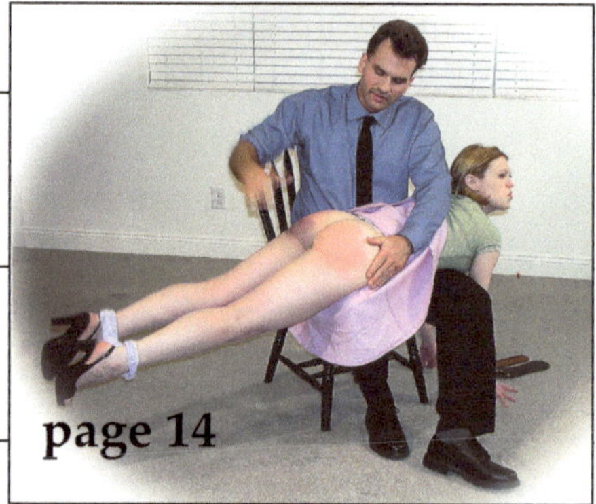
page 14

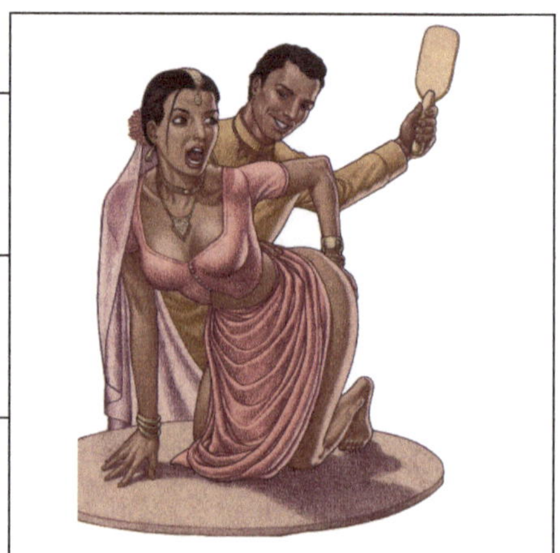
page 28

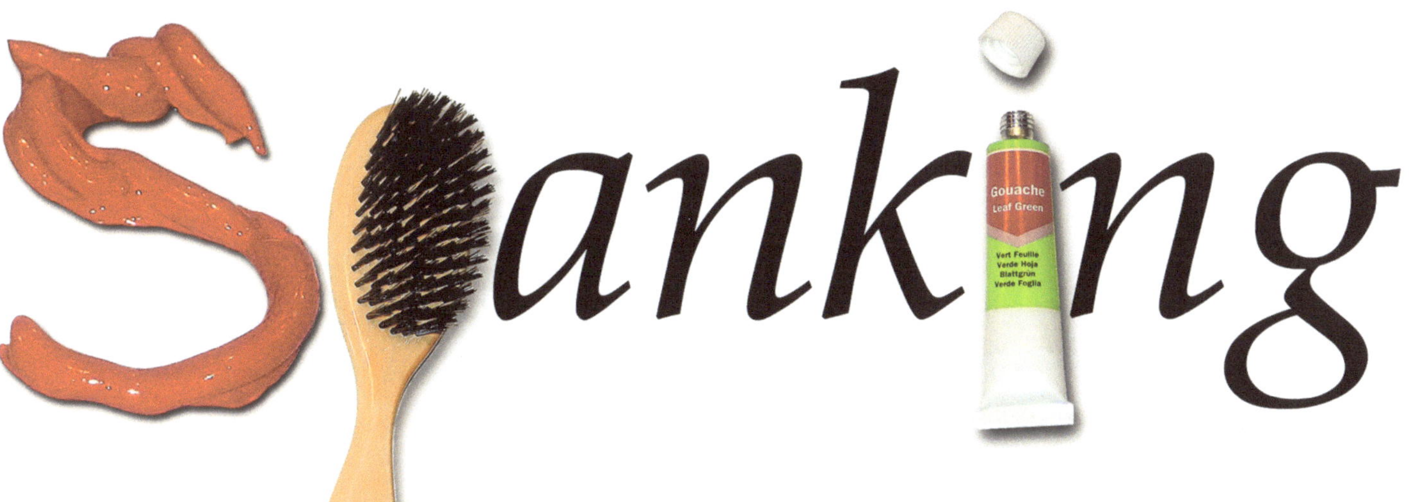

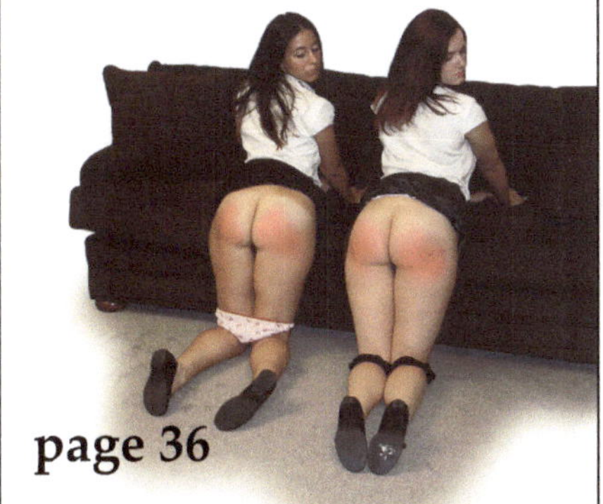
page 36

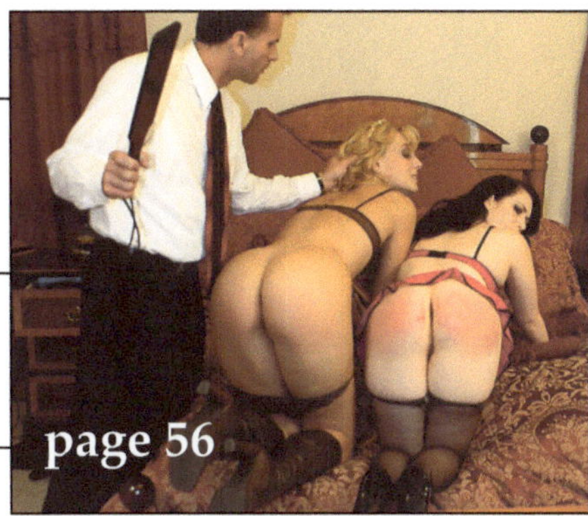
page 56

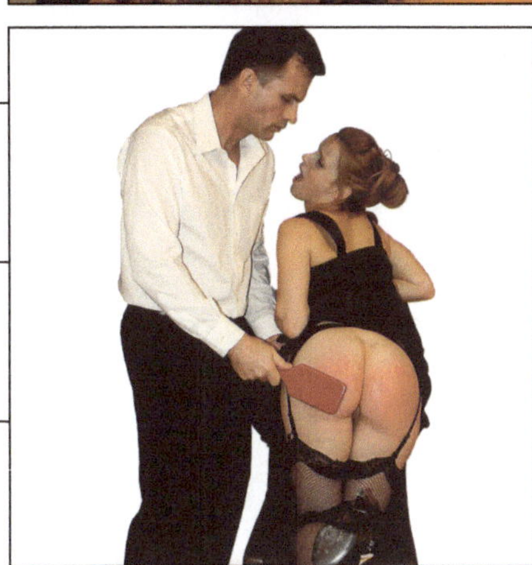
page 63

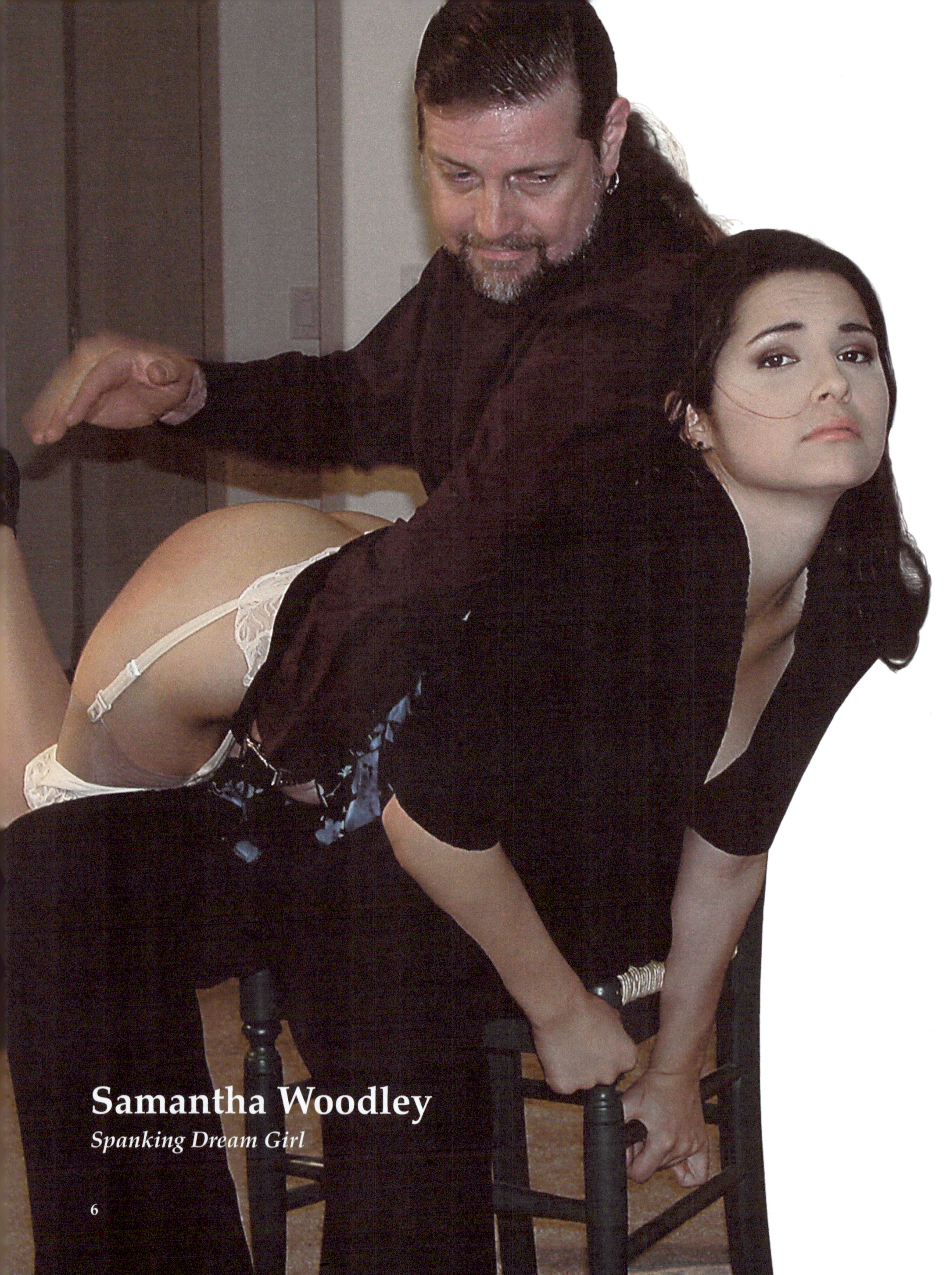

Samantha Woodley

Spanking Dream Girl

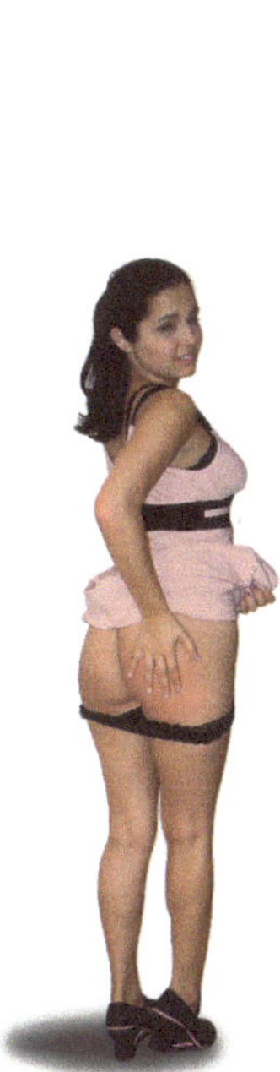

Opposite
Samantha co-starred with preeminent spanking illustrator and popular Shadow Lane actor Brian Tarsis in our video The Art of Spanking. In the 21st century real nylon stockings are harder and harder to find. Samantha's are held up with a cream lace garter belt, with the matching full panties pulled down to reveal one of the most callipygous backsides of the modern era, kissed with a stinging blush from the palm of Brian's very hard hand.

Right
Bewitchingly beautiful young Samantha Woodley may be separated from veteran spanker Keith Jones by a whole generation in years, but her integrity as a lifelong spanking enthusiast is every bit as deep and real as that of her unflappable dominant. Samantha Woodley is one of us and always has been and that is why we love her so.

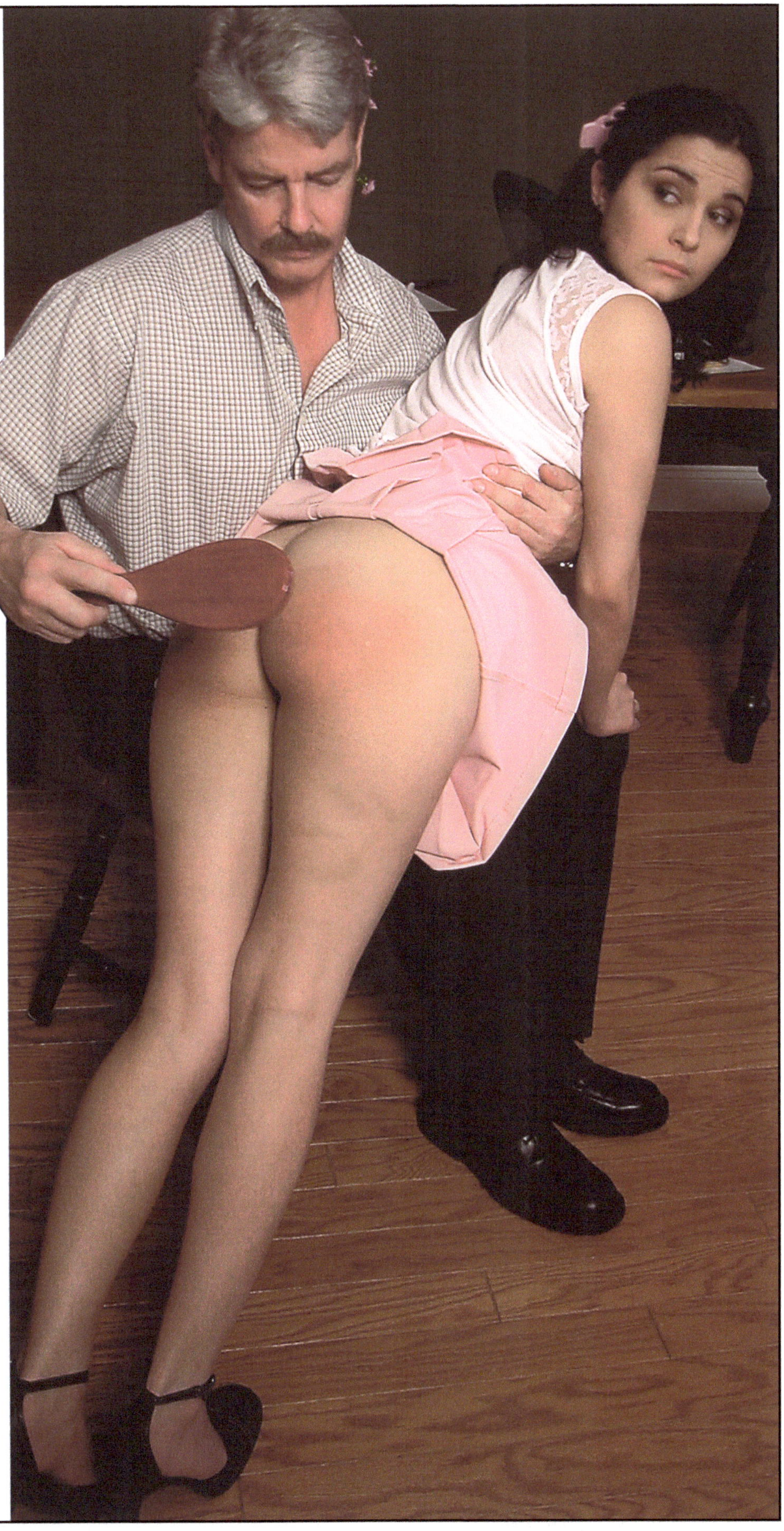

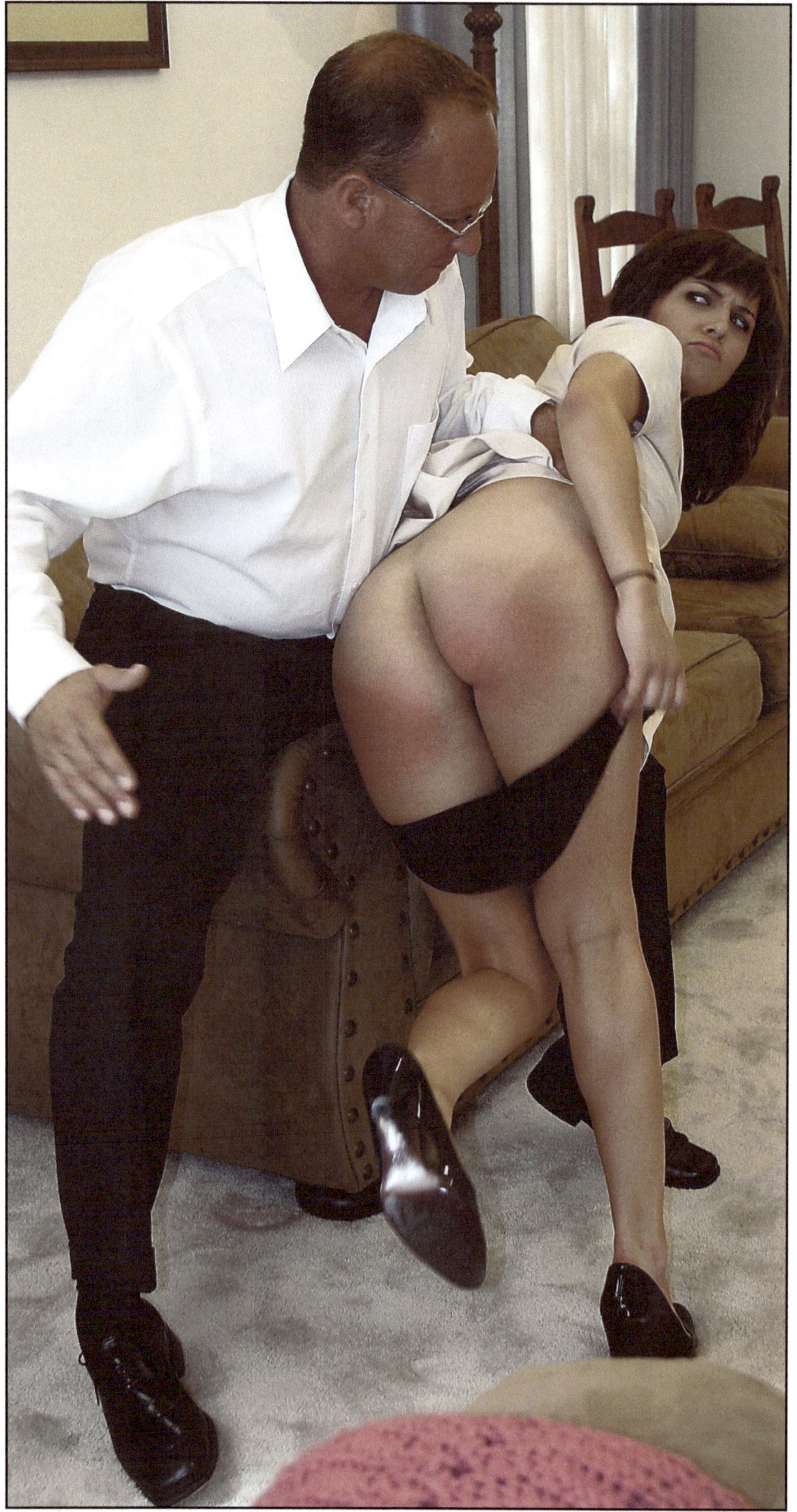

Left
Samantha expresses outrage at having her black panties unceremoniously yanked down by Lance del Toro. Many spankers fetish tan lines for a variety of reasons. First, they are cute, secondly, they suggest a sun warmed bottom wrapped in but a tiny bikini and thirdly, they create the illusion of being dressed and undressed at the same time.

Opposite
Samantha Woodley was only nineteen when she made her spanking video debut with Shadow Lane. She is pictured here in her first video, across the lap of the handsome and skillful Gino Coletti, who is himself a lifelong enthusiast.

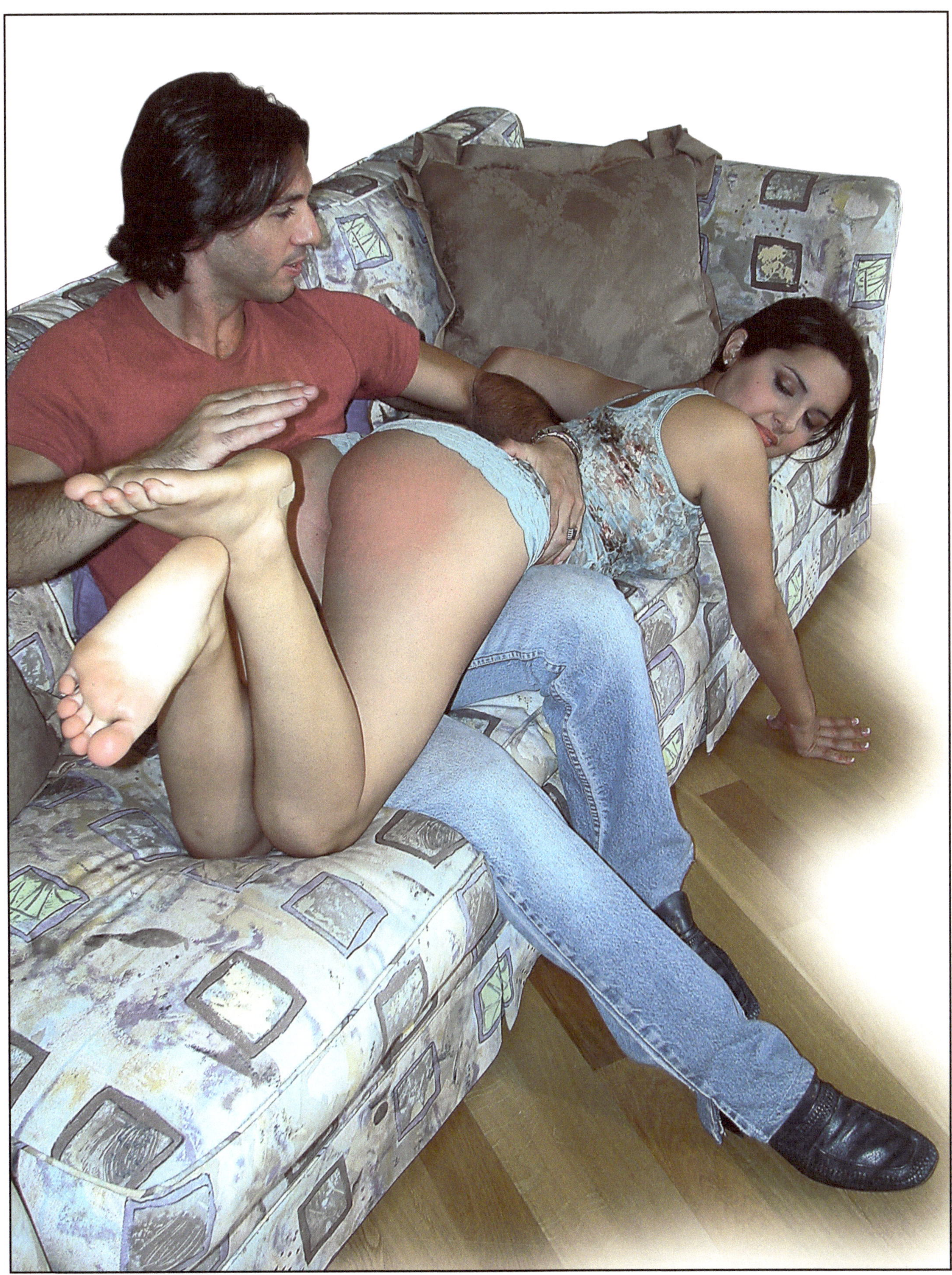

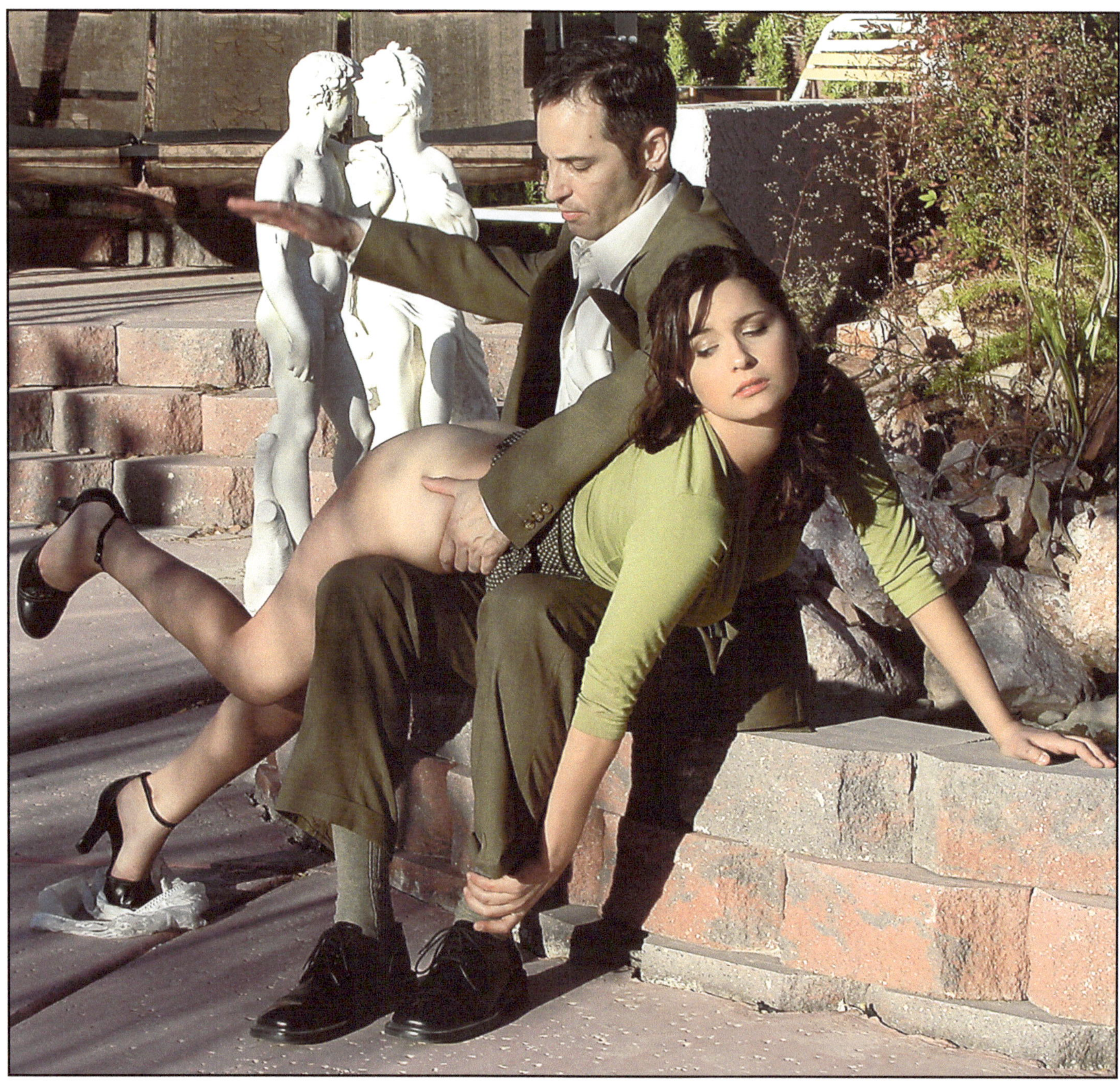

Besides being remarkably good looking and a complete spanking fetishist, Samantha is a quick witted and challenging brat, ready with a bright comeback to every lecture, often calculated, whether consciously or not, to earn her even more over the knee discipline. The chemistry between Samantha Woodley and handsome Arthur Sire has always been blazing hot.

Steve Fuller is just the right age, size and shape to fit into an idealized "young daddy" fantasy. But more than that, he knows how to hold, how to spank and how to scold. There is an art to taking control of a tender girl and visiting real corporal punishment on her bare skin. The object is to control yet excite the compliant but cautious submissive. The most popular dominant men master their women not with ferocity, but finesse.

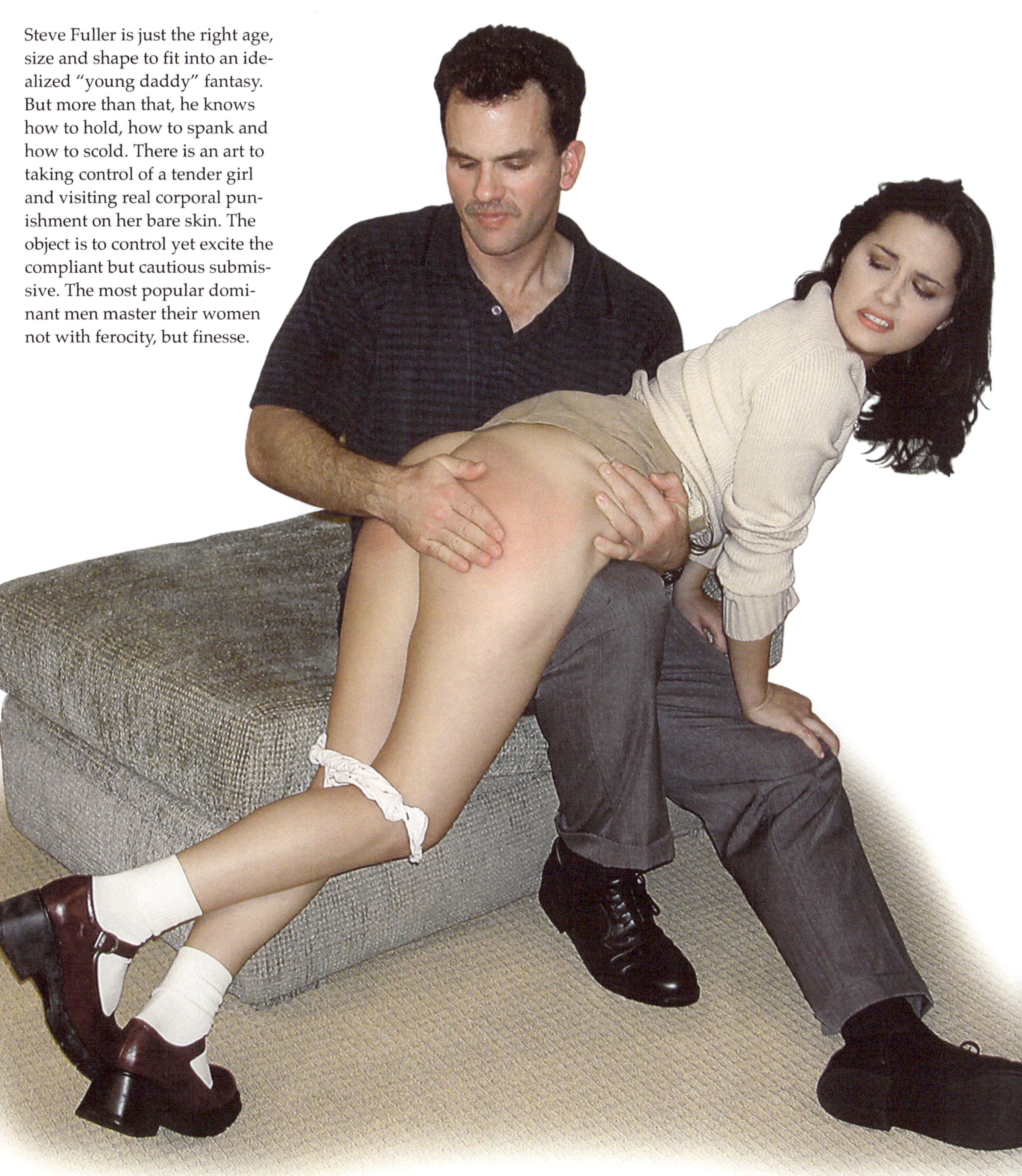

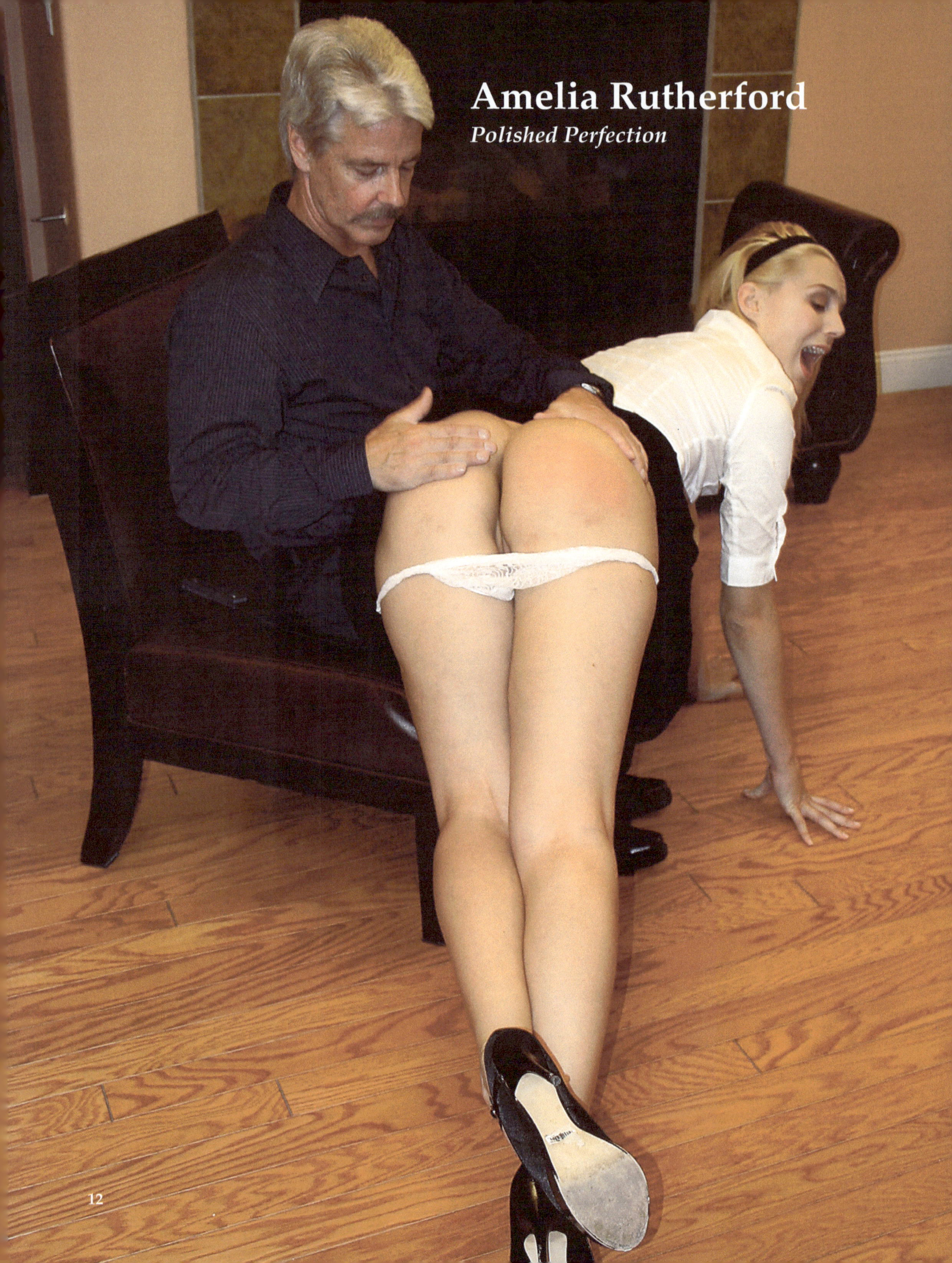

Amelia Rutherford

Polished Perfection

Opposite
Amelia Rutherford has been called "the Julie Andrews" of the spanking scene. It isn't just her Mayfair accent, radiant demeanor and elegant bearing, the lovely Londoner simply exudes good humor, good sportsmanship and enthusiasm. A former ballet dancer and actress, Amelia stands about 6′2″ tall and is as physically graceful as she is intellectually astute. Elegantly educated, with a delightful sense of humor, Amelia is well rounded in every possible way and incidentally, both takes and gives a great spanking!

Below
In the two part video "As Tears Go By" Amelia is spanked by Arthur Sire in Part 1 and Keith Jones in Part 2 of this tale of a hapless music teacher who gets into trouble with both her supervisor and her pupil's father for paddling his daughter without his consent. Keith demonstrates to the tender and sensitive Amelia that the art of caning is also practiced with due diligence in America.

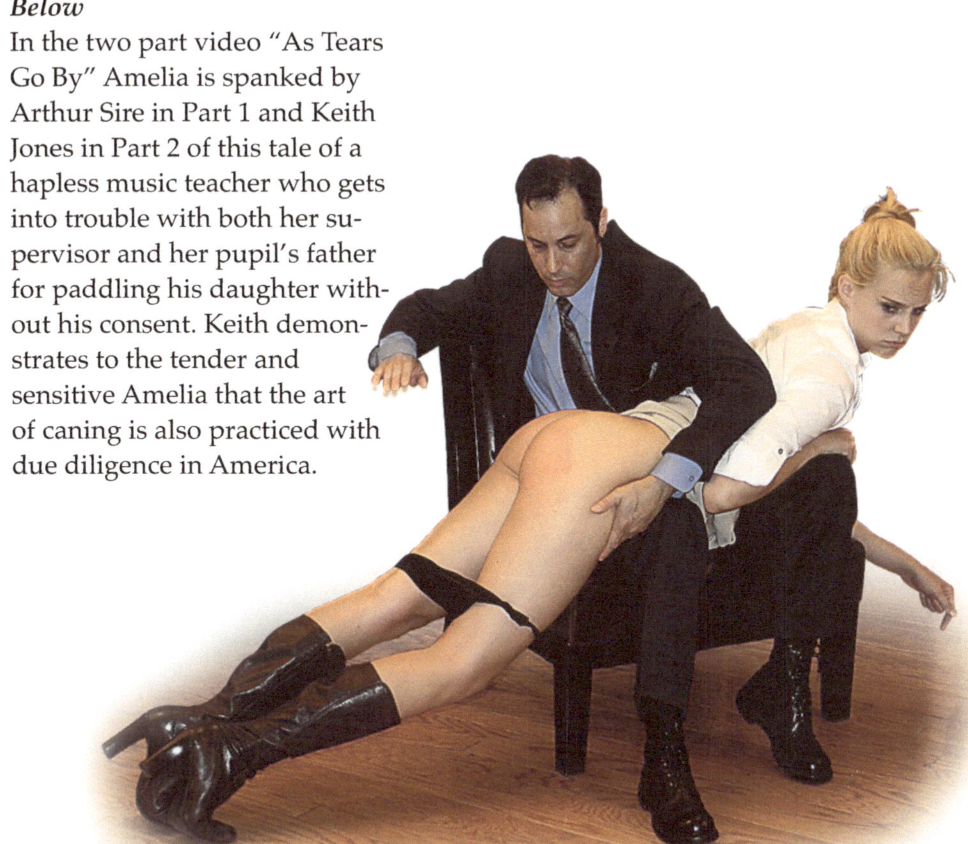

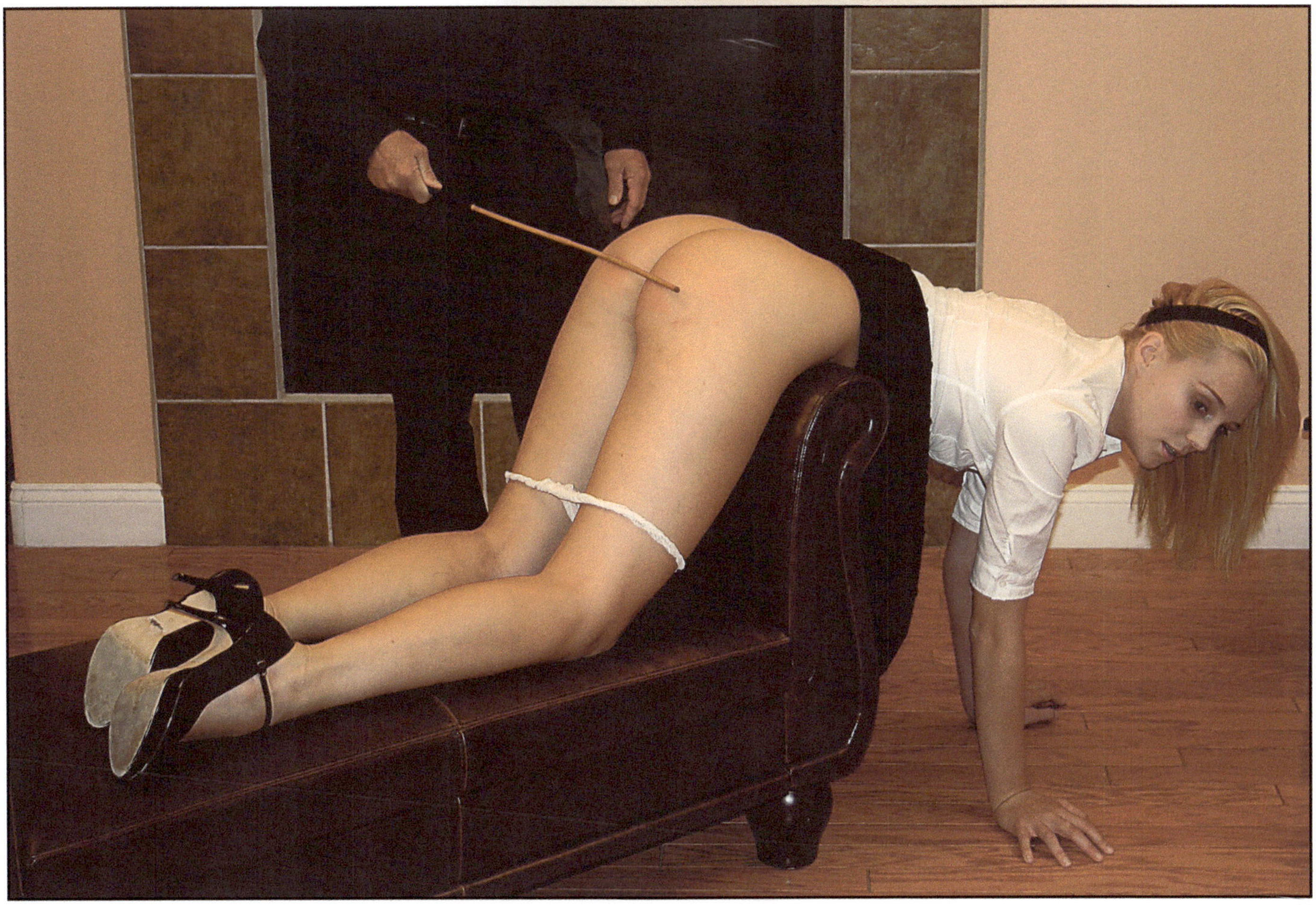

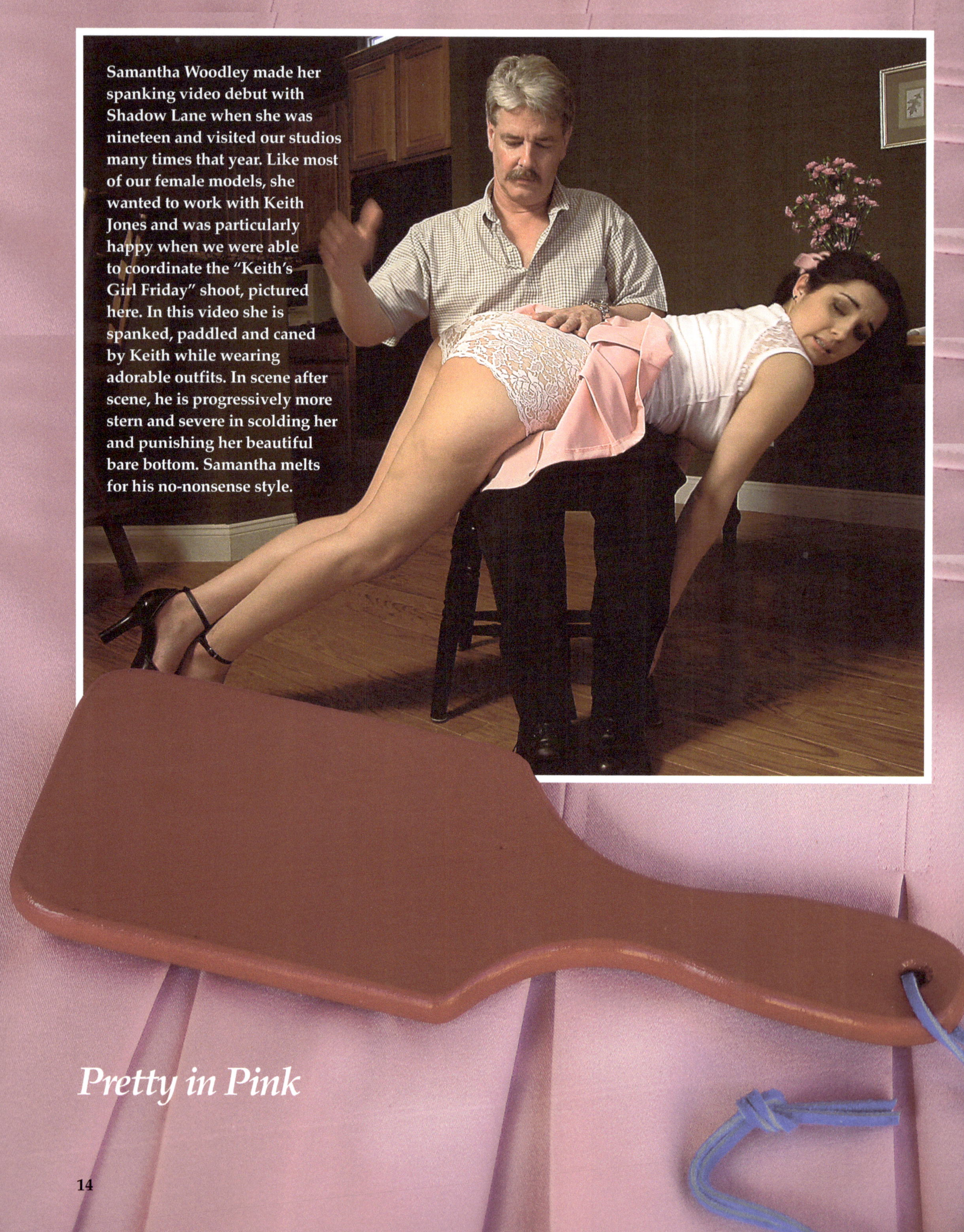

Samantha Woodley made her spanking video debut with Shadow Lane when she was nineteen and visited our studios many times that year. Like most of our female models, she wanted to work with Keith Jones and was particularly happy when we were able to coordinate the "Keith's Girl Friday" shoot, pictured here. In this video she is spanked, paddled and caned by Keith while wearing adorable outfits. In scene after scene, he is progressively more stern and severe in scolding her and punishing her beautiful bare bottom. Samantha melts for his no-nonsense style.

Pretty in Pink

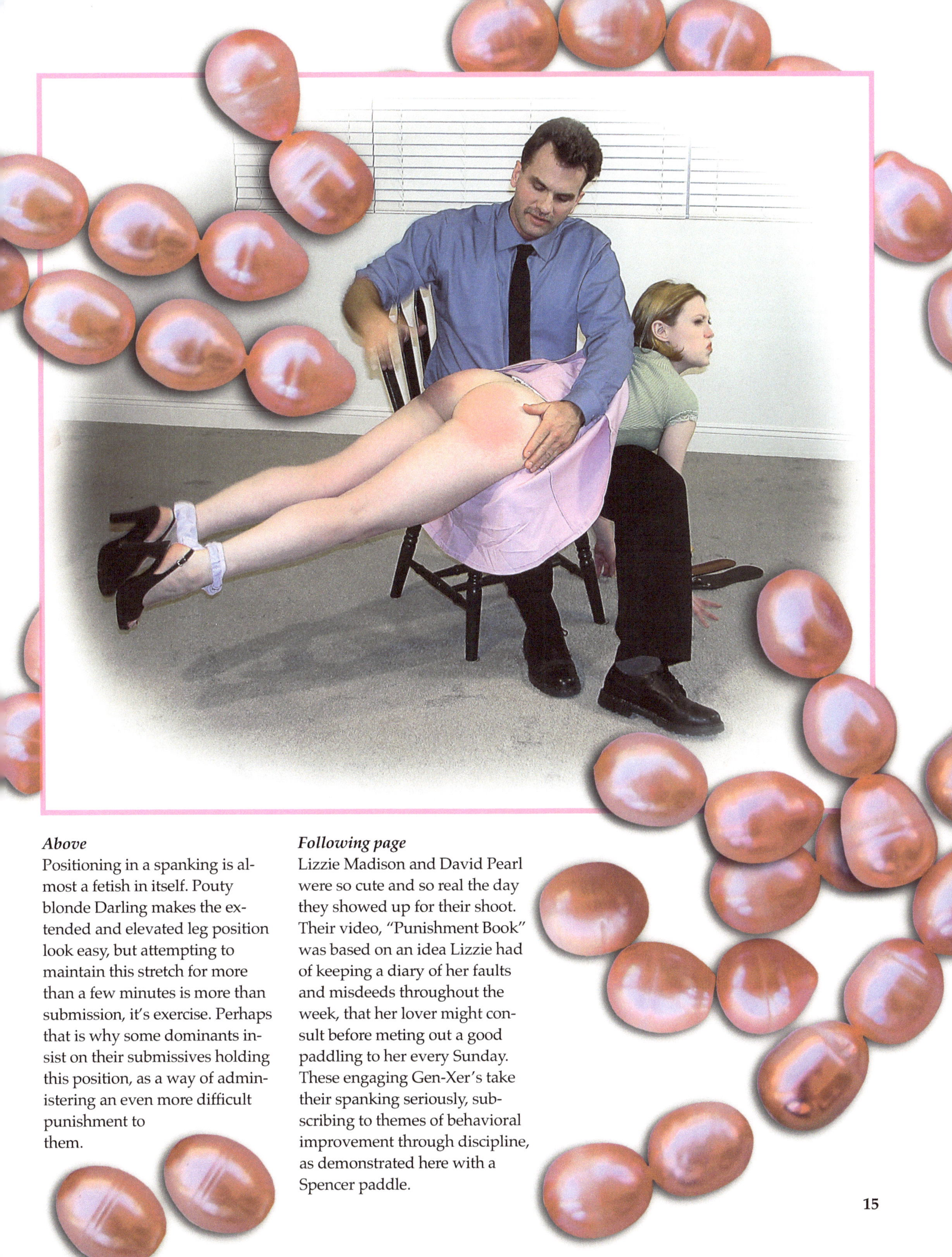

Above
Positioning in a spanking is almost a fetish in itself. Pouty blonde Darling makes the extended and elevated leg position look easy, but attempting to maintain this stretch for more than a few minutes is more than submission, it's exercise. Perhaps that is why some dominants insist on their submissives holding this position, as a way of administering an even more difficult punishment to them.

Following page
Lizzie Madison and David Pearl were so cute and so real the day they showed up for their shoot. Their video, "Punishment Book" was based on an idea Lizzie had of keeping a diary of her faults and misdeeds throughout the week, that her lover might consult before meting out a good paddling to her every Sunday. These engaging Gen-Xer's take their spanking seriously, subscribing to themes of behavioral improvement through discipline, as demonstrated here with a Spencer paddle.

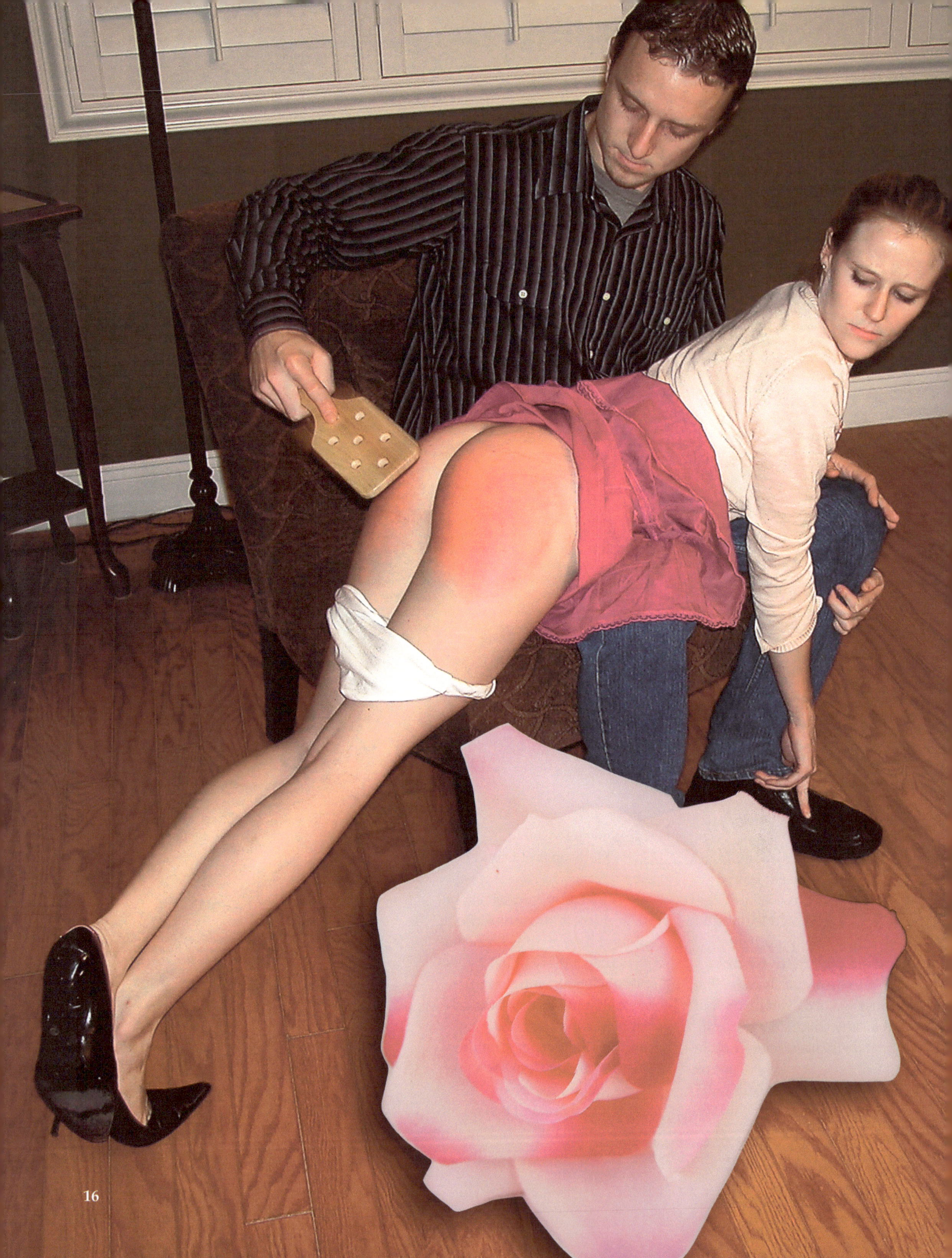

Women Who Spank Women

Women who spank women don't particularly care if you think of them as bossy or domineering and actually cultivate these traits in order to become more effective disciplinarians. Female spankers consider it their duty to administer serious corporal punishment to those in need of it and subsequently bask in the respect that is their due.

The daintily shapely Sinn Sage spanks Lena Ramone's bare bottom in a scene from "Our Sorority Punishment Parade".

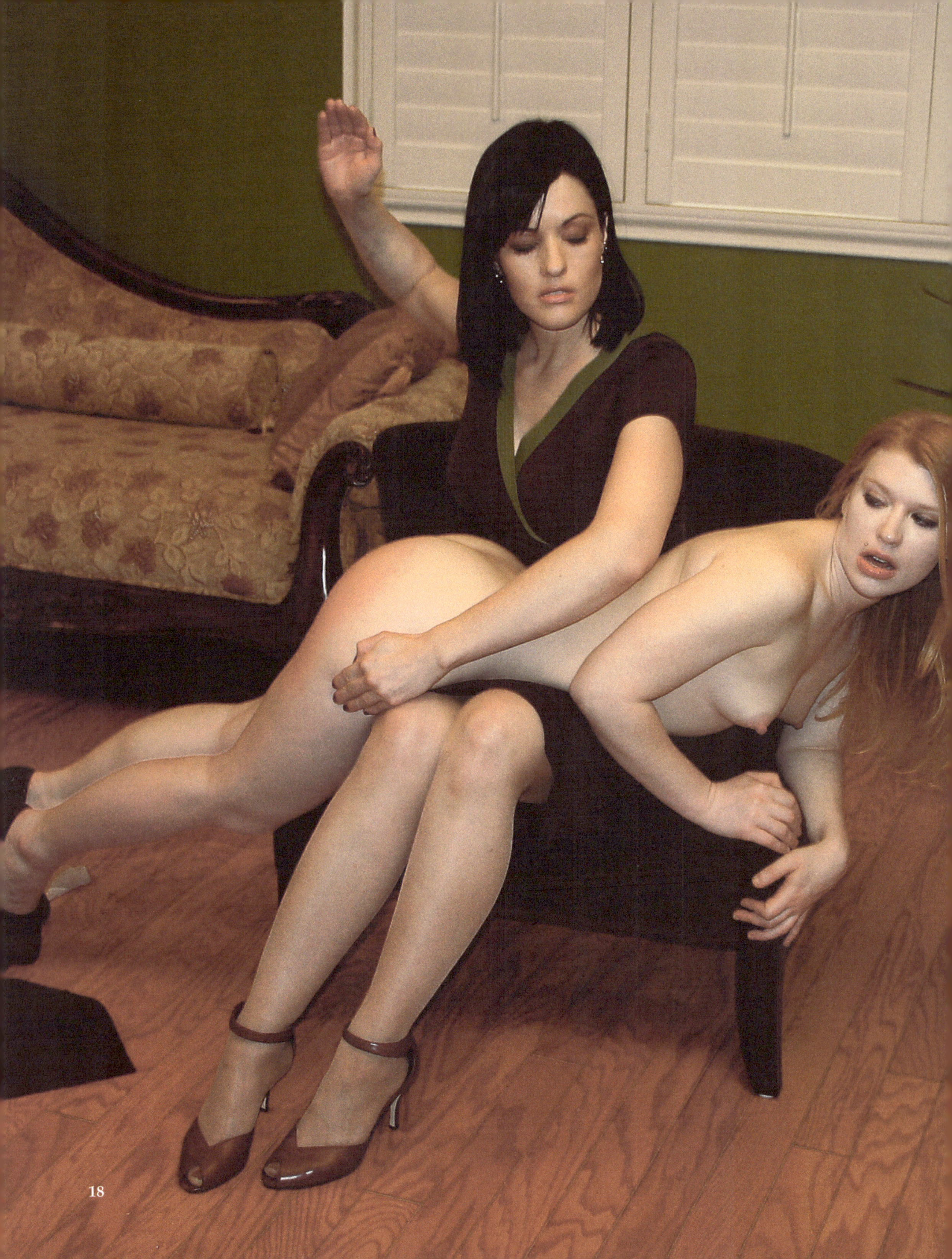

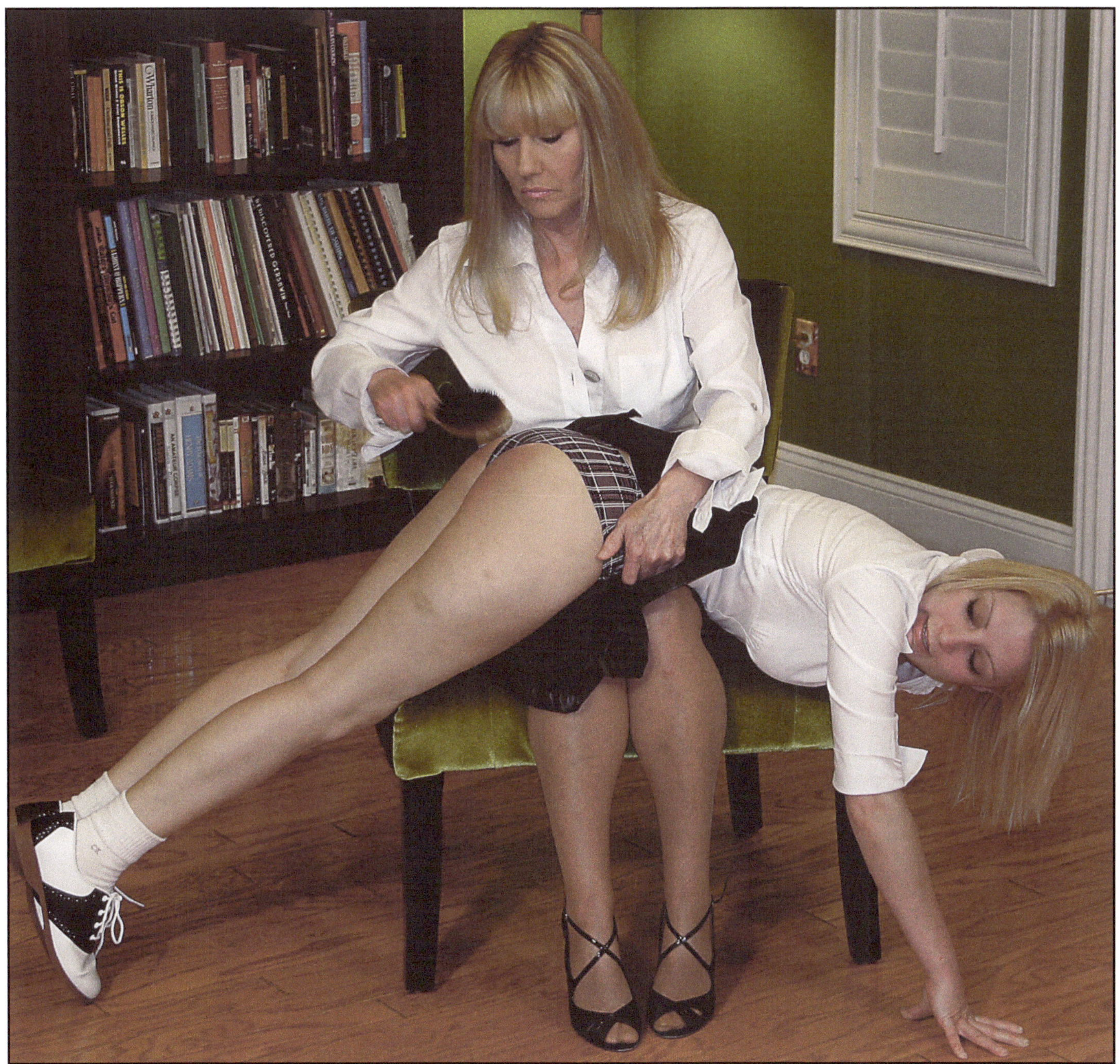

Opposite page
Versatile Snow overwhelms the lusciously nude Madison Young with a traditional hand spanking in the sensational warm up scene from "Spanking Girl's Back Door Man".

Above
In this scene from "Brat Whack" Gretta Carlson spanks her fresh and idle coed daughter Kat St. James with a wooden hairbrush.

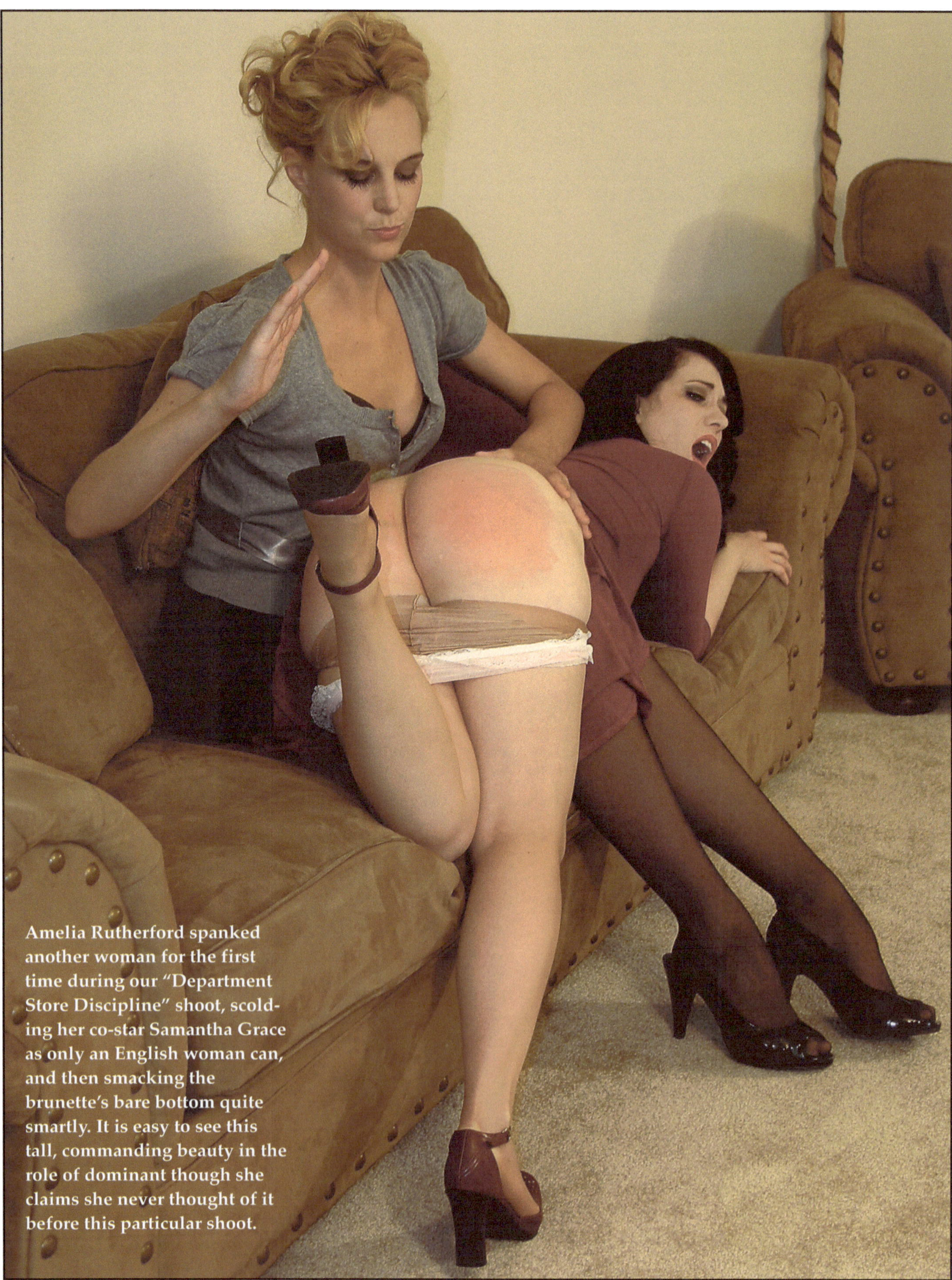

Amelia Rutherford spanked another woman for the first time during our "Department Store Discipline" shoot, scolding her co-star Samantha Grace as only an English woman can, and then smacking the brunette's bare bottom quite smartly. It is easy to see this tall, commanding beauty in the role of dominant though she claims she never thought of it before this particular shoot.

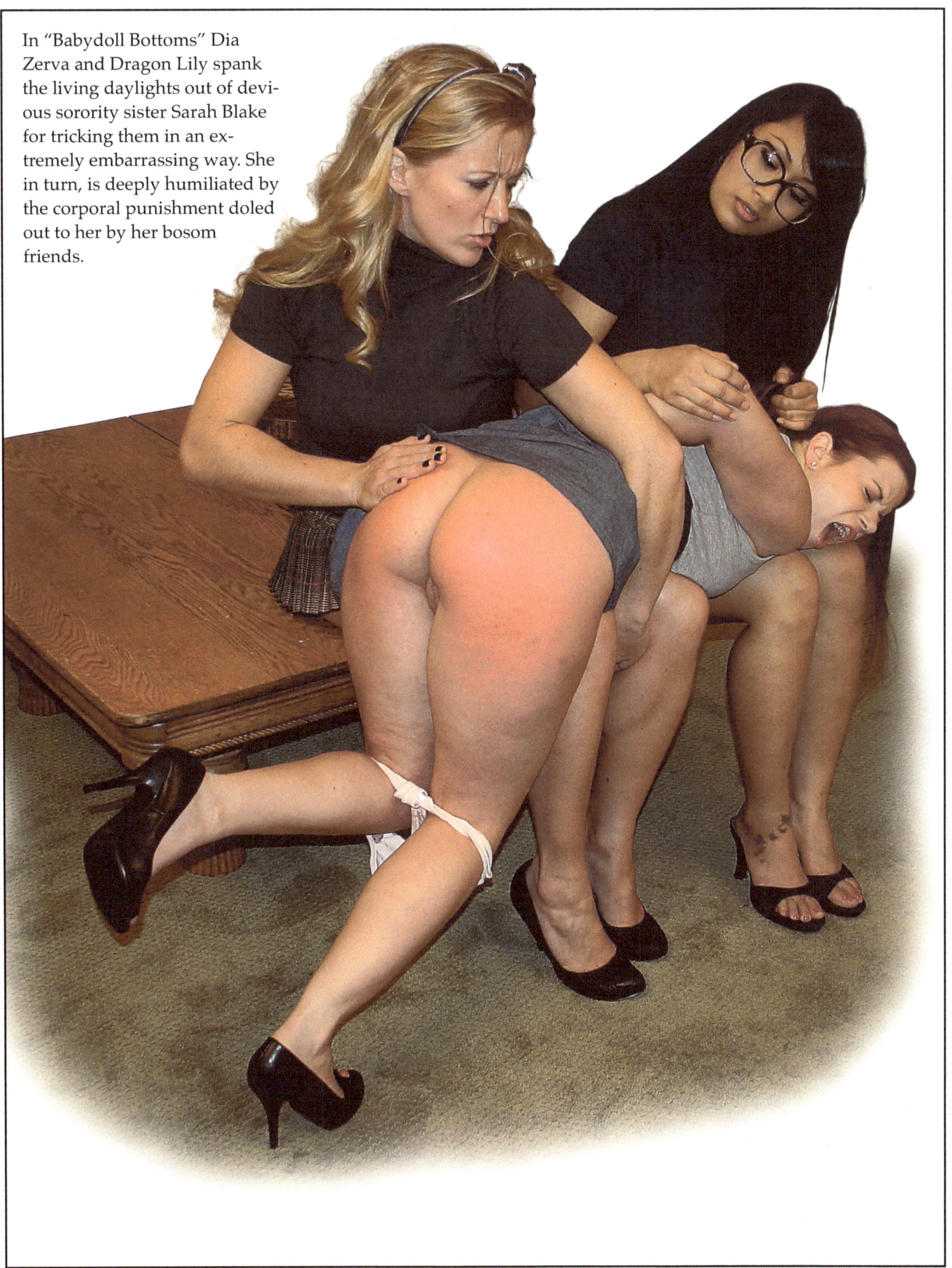

In "Babydoll Bottoms" Dia Zerva and Dragon Lily spank the living daylights out of devious sorority sister Sarah Blake for tricking them in an extremely embarrassing way. She in turn, is deeply humiliated by the corporal punishment doled out to her by her bosom friends.

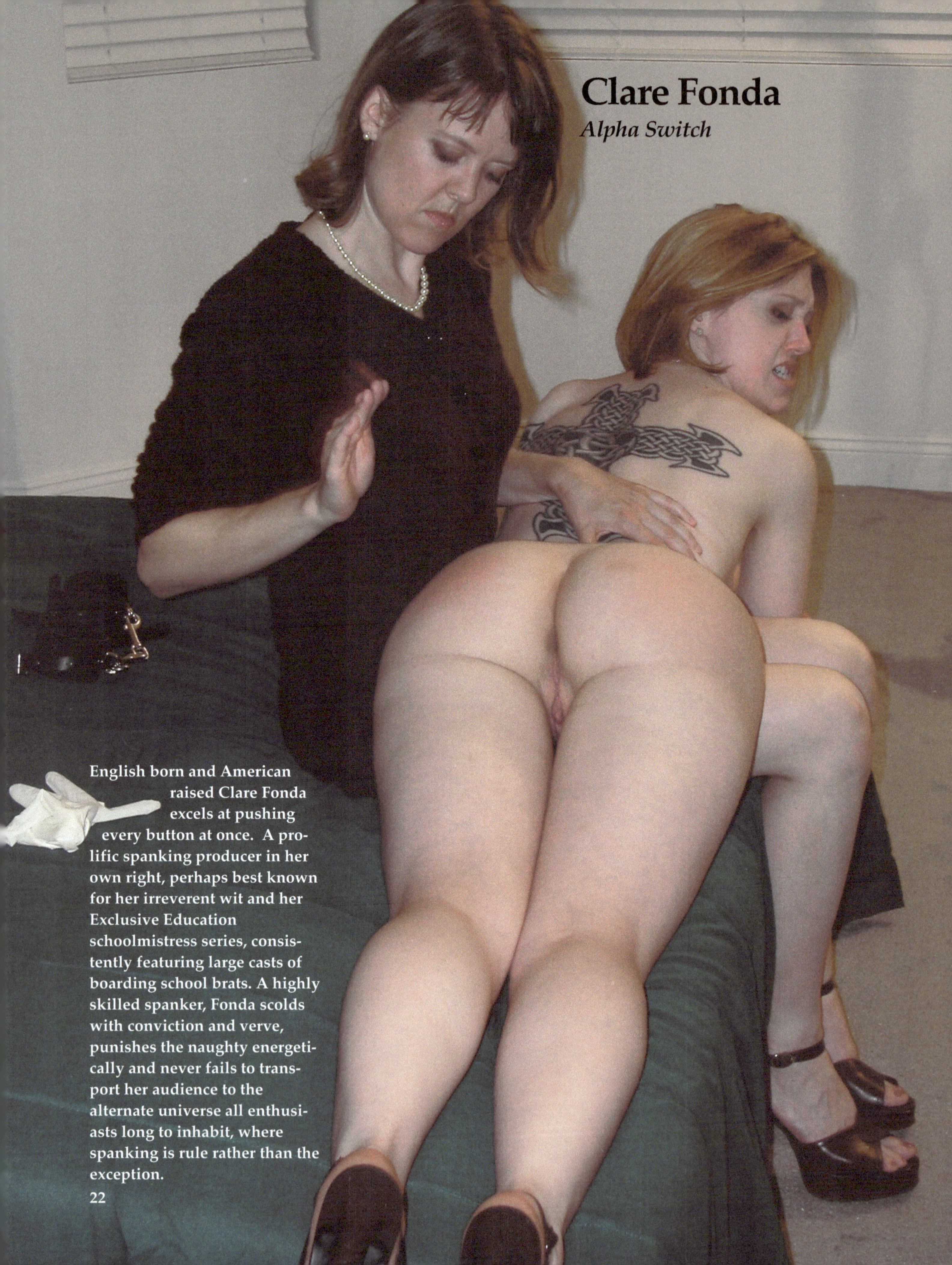

Clare Fonda

Alpha Switch

English born and American raised Clare Fonda excels at pushing every button at once. A prolific spanking producer in her own right, perhaps best known for her irreverent wit and her Exclusive Education schoolmistress series, consistently featuring large casts of boarding school brats. A highly skilled spanker, Fonda scolds with conviction and verve, punishes the naughty energetically and never fails to transport her audience to the alternate universe all enthusiasts long to inhabit, where spanking is rule rather than the exception.

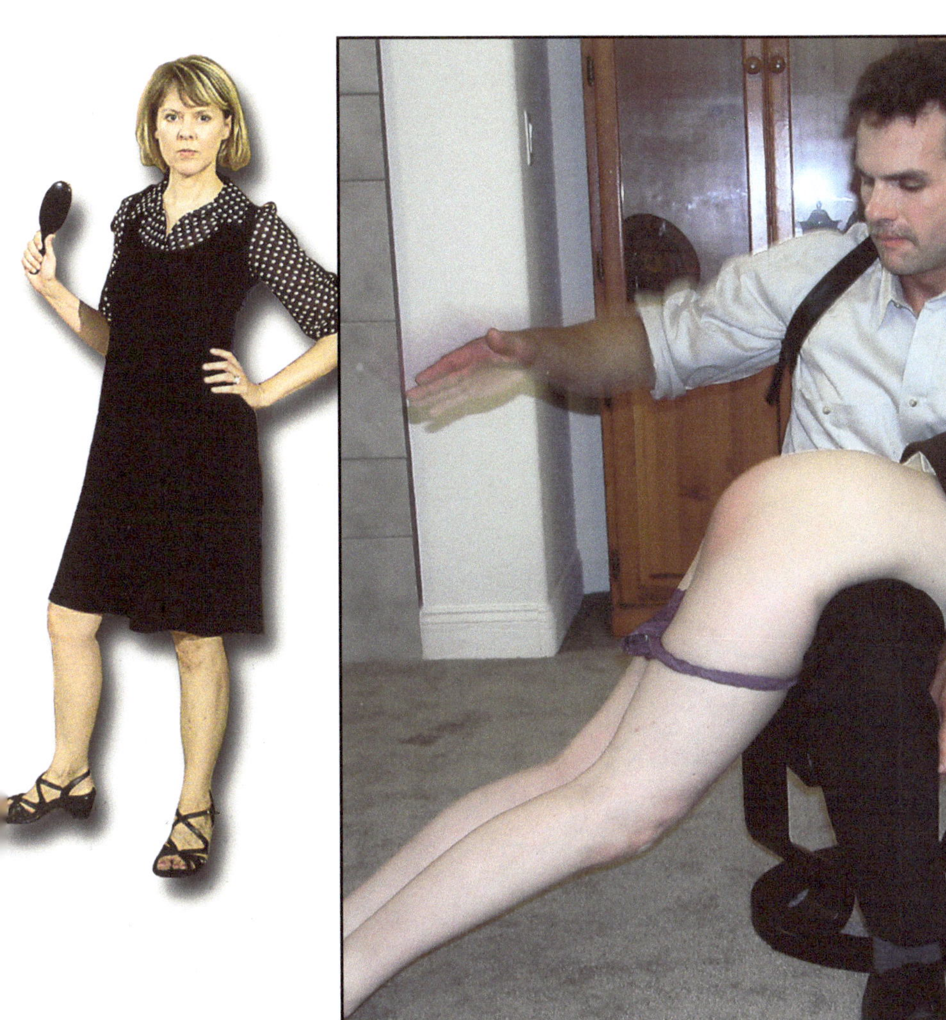

Opposite page
This is the first scene Clare ever shot for Shadow Lane and it is a knockout. She is spanking Darling, a very charming Texas girl, whom she brought to our studios to co-star with herself and Steve Fuller in "Good Cop Bad Cop", a modern spanking police drama. Within the scenario, Darling is the criminal informant interrogated by Fonda in the unorthodox manner portrayed.

Above
For bungling their stakeout and abusing their informant, Fuller, the "good" cop punishes Fonda, the "bad" cop in traditional style. Clare has the unusual ability to cry on camera and did so in this scene.

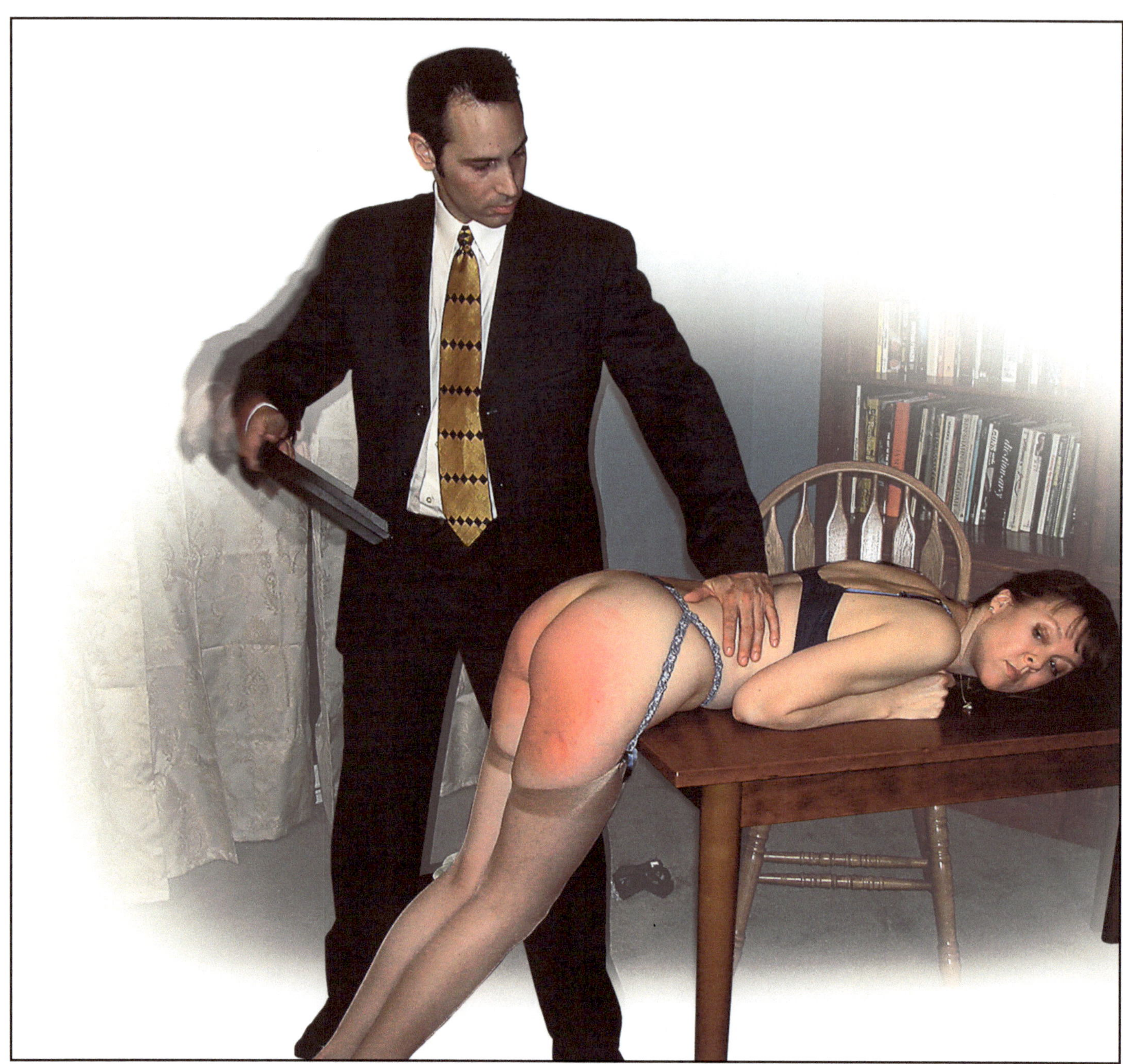

Not a spanking fetishist by orientation, Fonda nevertheless possesses an uncanny, intuitive understanding of the spanking fetish that sets her apart. An exacting and critical top, she is conversely, a softly feminine bottom; compliant, conciliatory, wriggling, wheedling and ultimately vulnerable. In both guises, the irreverent spanking auteur is a captivating performer who time after time demonstrates the acuity to write better lines for herself than anyone else ever could. Fonda has starred in many Shadow Lane videos. In this scene from "Prep School Punishments" Clare plays a sexy instructress who is disciplined by Headmaster Arthur Sire for encouraging erections in the senior boys.

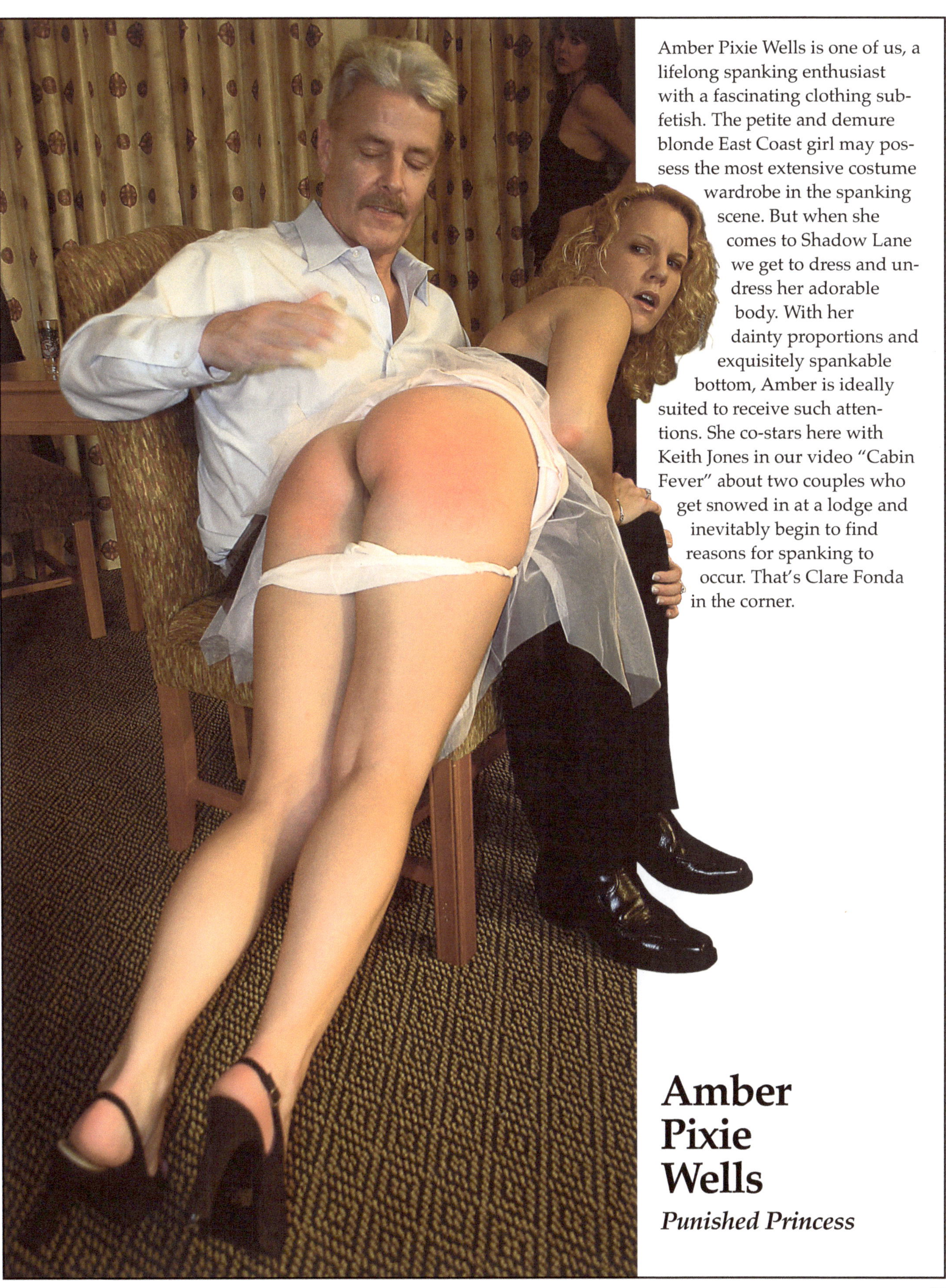

Amber Pixie Wells is one of us, a lifelong spanking enthusiast with a fascinating clothing sub-fetish. The petite and demure blonde East Coast girl may possess the most extensive costume wardrobe in the spanking scene. But when she comes to Shadow Lane we get to dress and undress her adorable body. With her dainty proportions and exquisitely spankable bottom, Amber is ideally suited to receive such attentions. She co-stars here with Keith Jones in our video "Cabin Fever" about two couples who get snowed in at a lodge and inevitably begin to find reasons for spanking to occur. That's Clare Fonda in the corner.

Amber Pixie Wells

Punished Princess

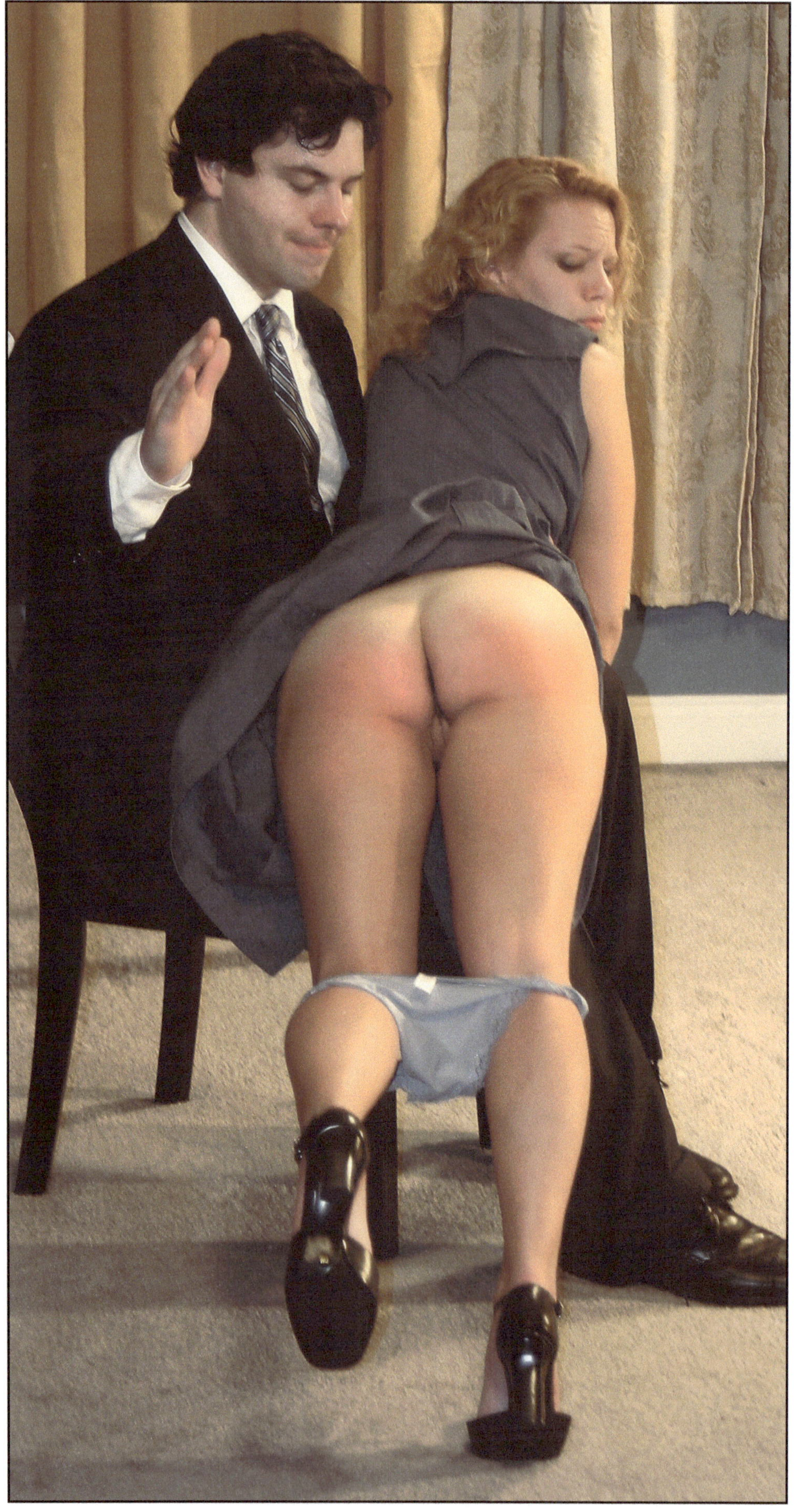

Amber is as truly amiable, not to mention genuinely well behaved, as her calm and graceful demeanor implies, but in spite of her irreproachable virtue, she can be a stubborn little goody two shoes, which often leads to people deciding to correct her. In this scene from "Heirs to Misfortune" she is spanked by her attorney, Mike Nous.

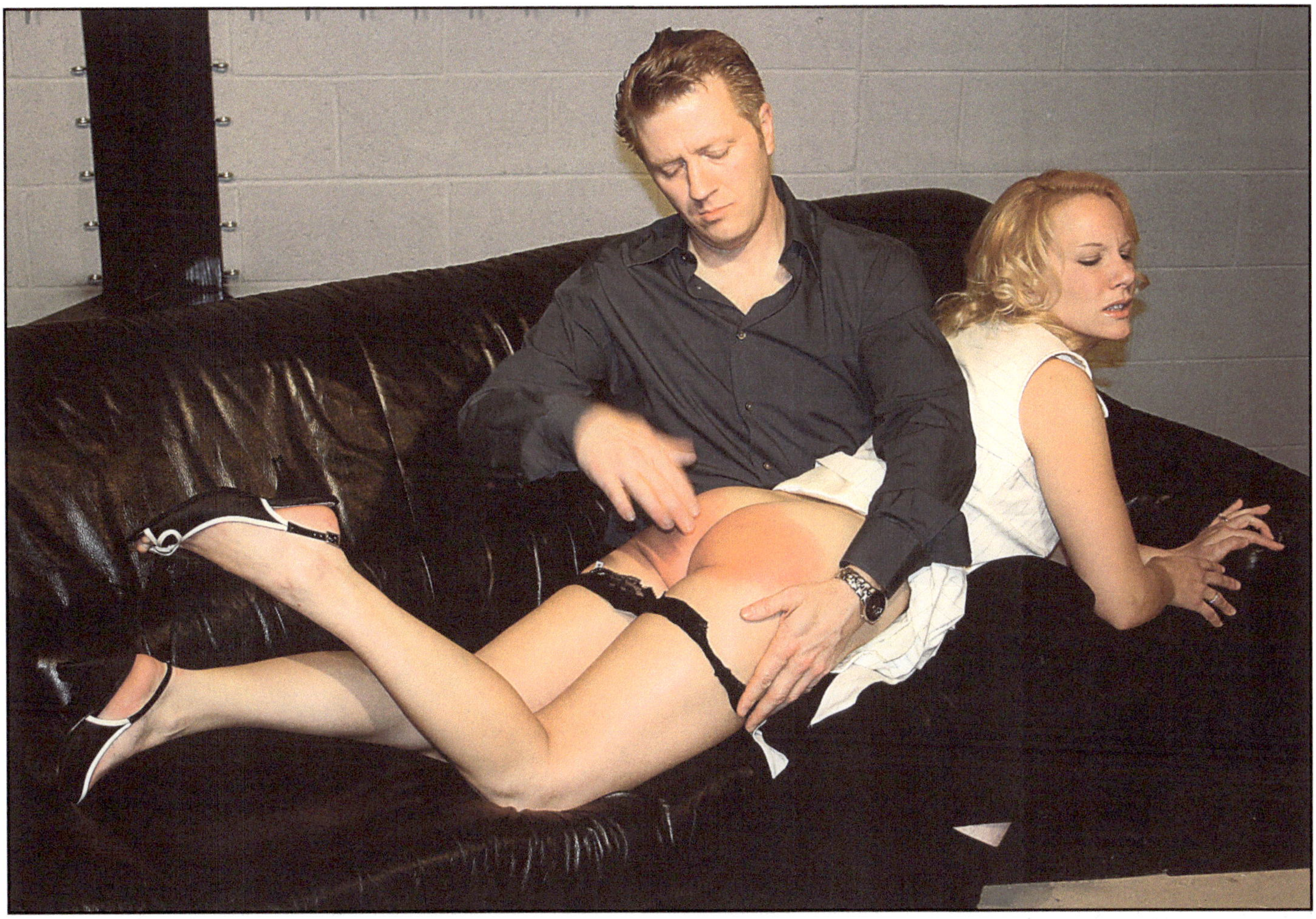

This outfit perfectly demonstrates the Amber paradox. White on top for innocence or at least, harmlessness, but underneath, extremely naughty, lace trimmed black panties. Girls in our scene learn quickly that men who spank like pulling down black panties. In this scene from "Dangerous Blondes" Amber has gone to clinical behaviorist Danny Chrighton to get the willfulness spanked out of her for her own good. (It is rare, but women sometimes do ask for spankings and in certain cases, even pay for them.) The therapy is said to be temporarily efficacious but seldom effects any lasting changes. Yet people into spanking want to believe.

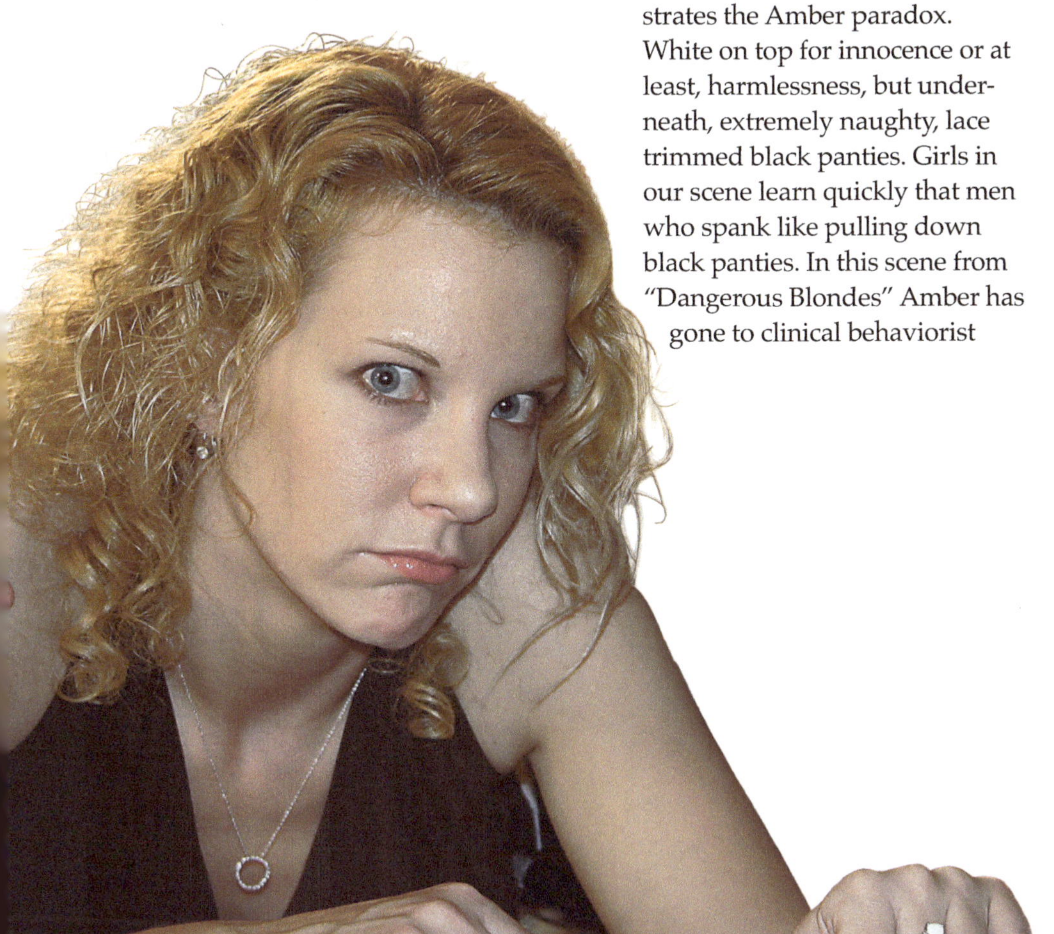

Tarsis Art Gallery

Brian Tarsis has been Shadow Lane's premiere illustrator for twenty years, his superb spanking drawings and cartoons lending a distinctive flair to our publications and website and helping us define the romance of discipline. Tarsis also drew all the cover art for the Shadow Lane novels by Eve Howard. A graphic novelist of distinction (Tarsis has authored City of Dreams, Valeria and other deliriously explicit B&D adventures), Brian has also starred in some of our most popular spanking videos, demonstrating his hands-on disciplinary and bondage skills with what could well be described as gusto. Join our members' clubhouse at www.shadowlane.com to view our entire collection of Tarsis art.

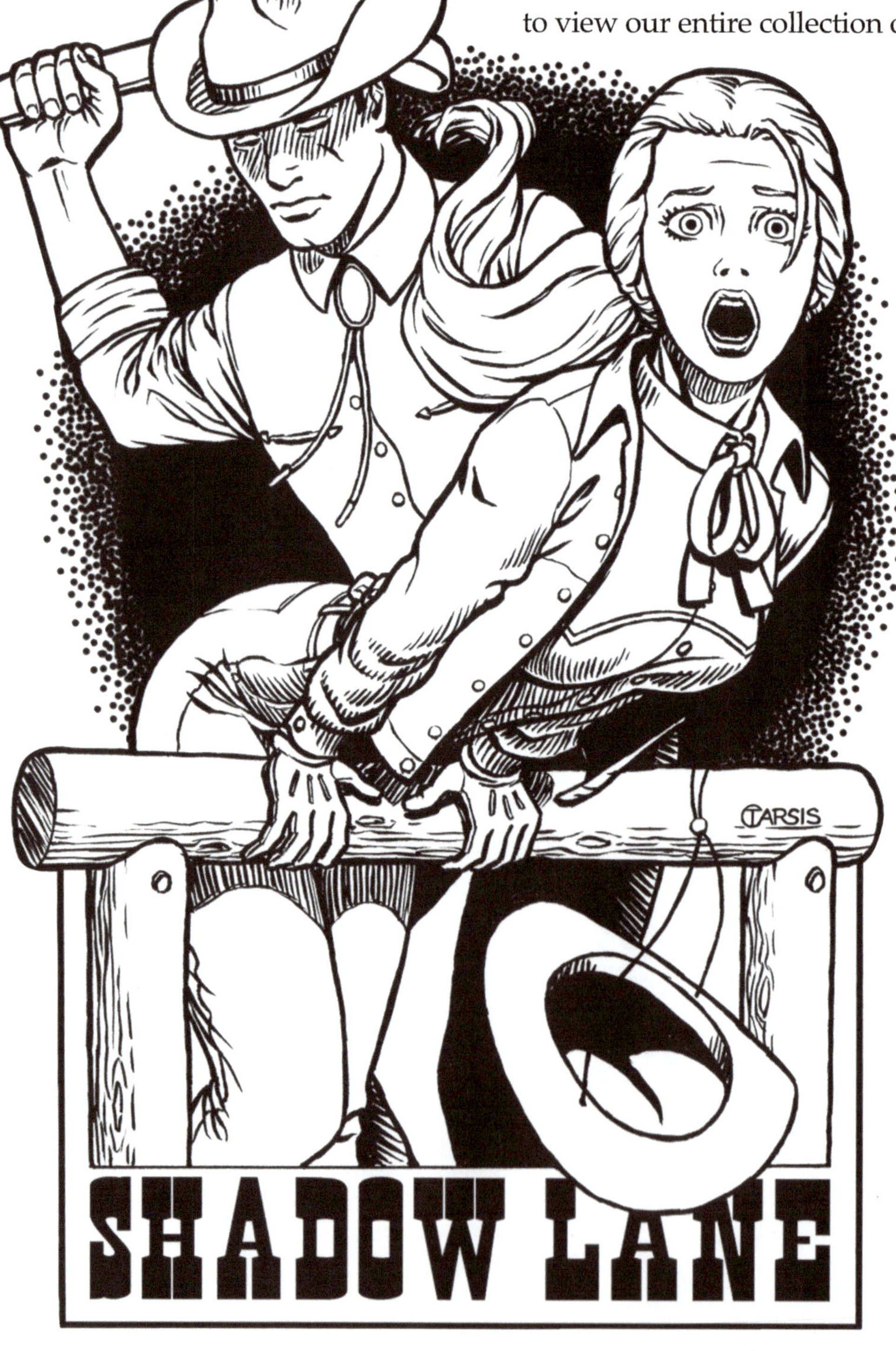

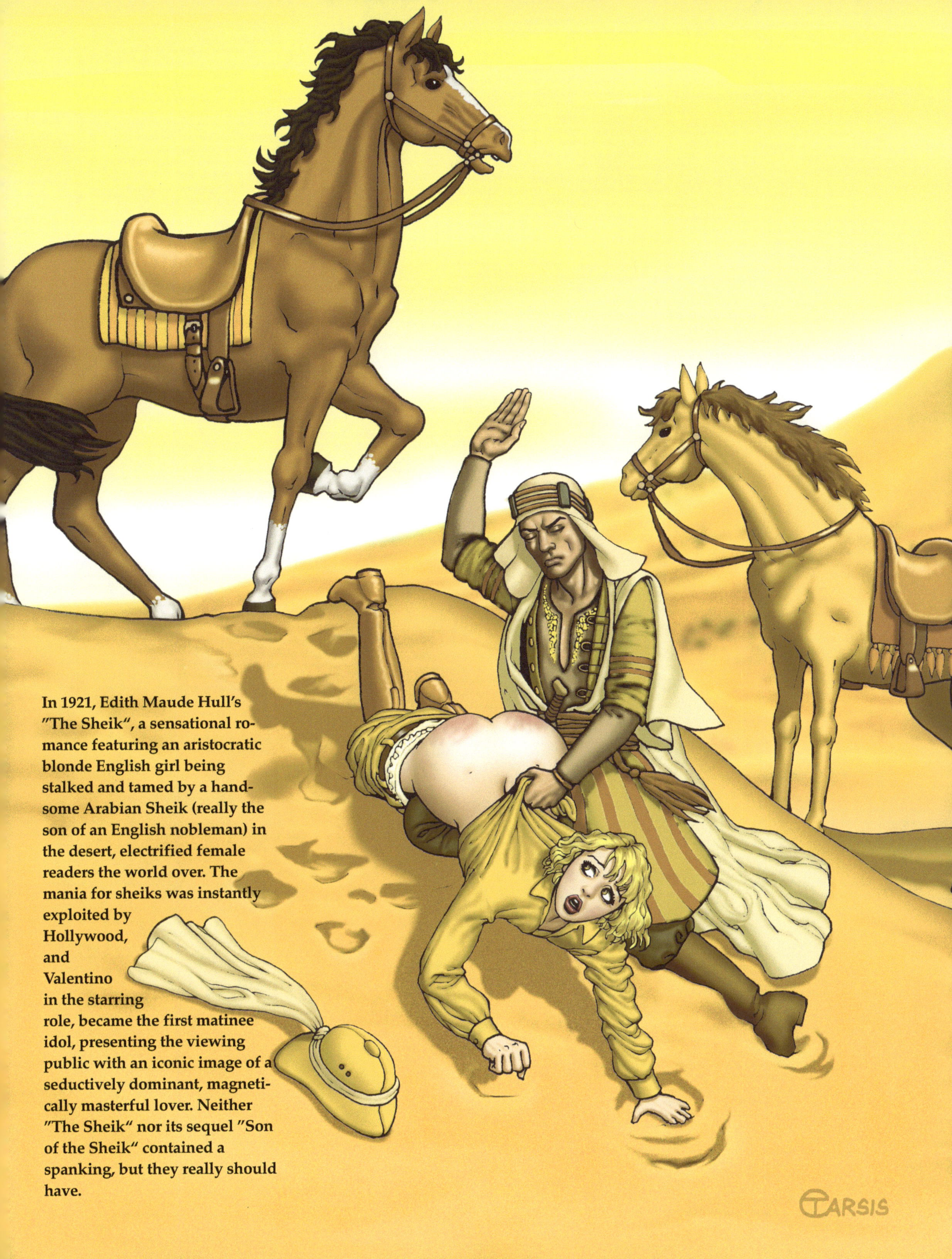

In 1921, Edith Maude Hull's "The Sheik", a sensational romance featuring an aristocratic blonde English girl being stalked and tamed by a handsome Arabian Sheik (really the son of an English nobleman) in the desert, electrified female readers the world over. The mania for sheiks was instantly exploited by Hollywood, and Valentino in the starring role, became the first matinee idol, presenting the viewing public with an iconic image of a seductively dominant, magnetically masterful lover. Neither "The Sheik" nor its sequel "Son of the Sheik" contained a spanking, but they really should have.

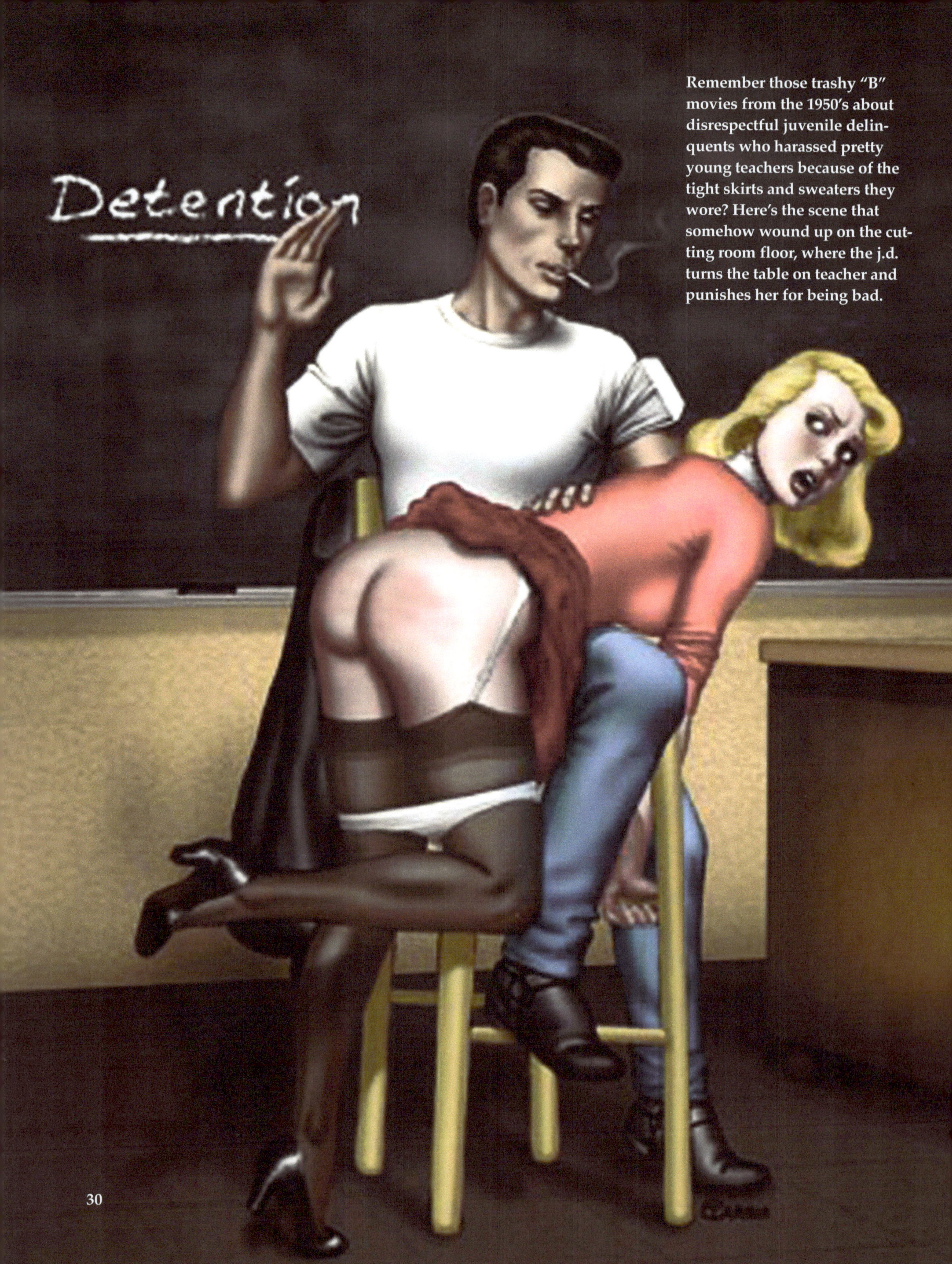

Remember those trashy "B" movies from the 1950's about disrespectful juvenile delinquents who harassed pretty young teachers because of the tight skirts and sweaters they wore? Here's the scene that somehow wound up on the cutting room floor, where the j.d. turns the table on teacher and punishes her for being bad.

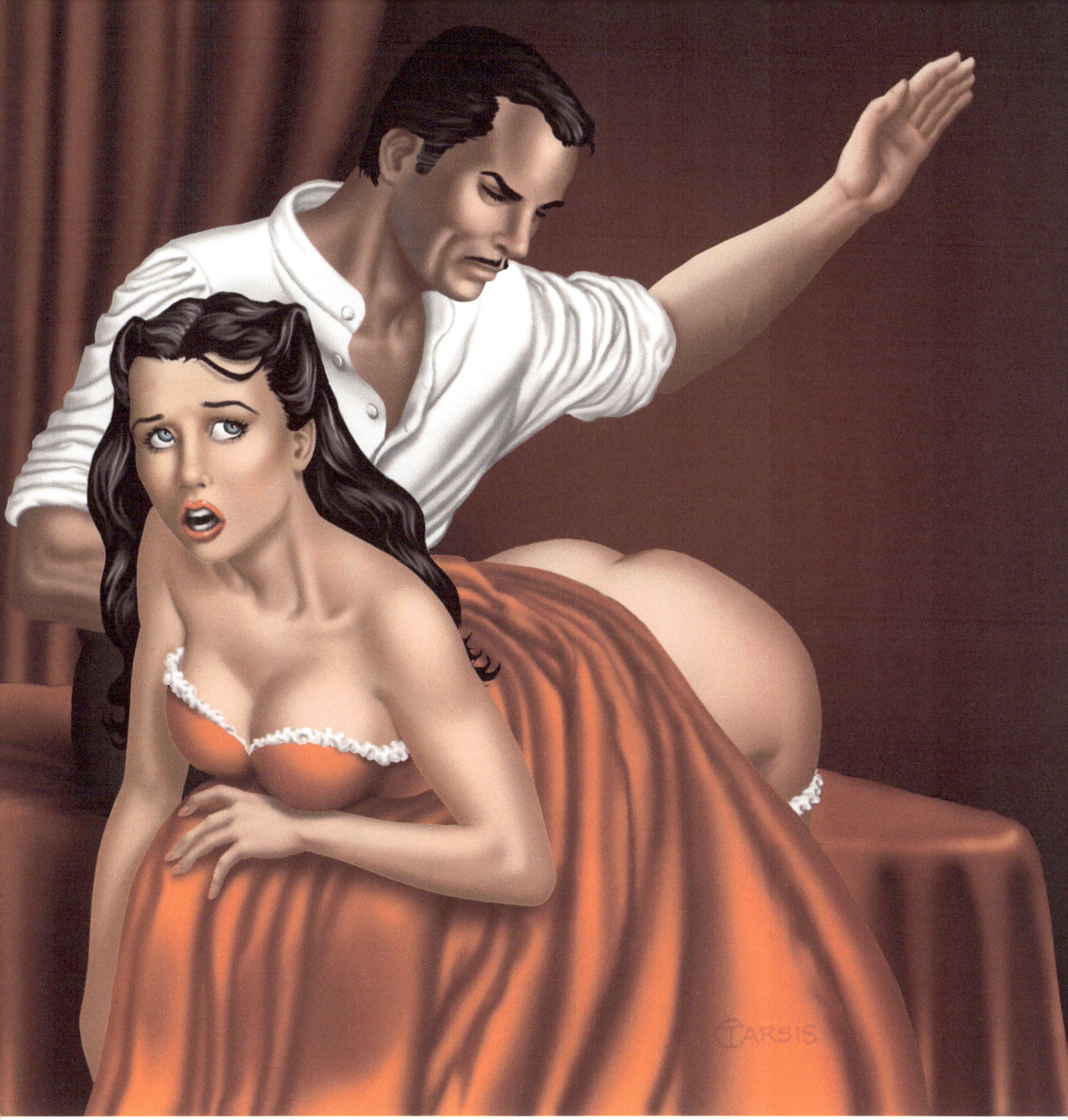

What actually happened when Rhett carried Scarlett up to their bedroom and kicked the door shut? We know that very hot sex transpired but would hope a little foreplay came first, possibly in the form of the spanking that she so deserved. Here Tarsis imagines the greatest spanking that never happened, from GWTW.

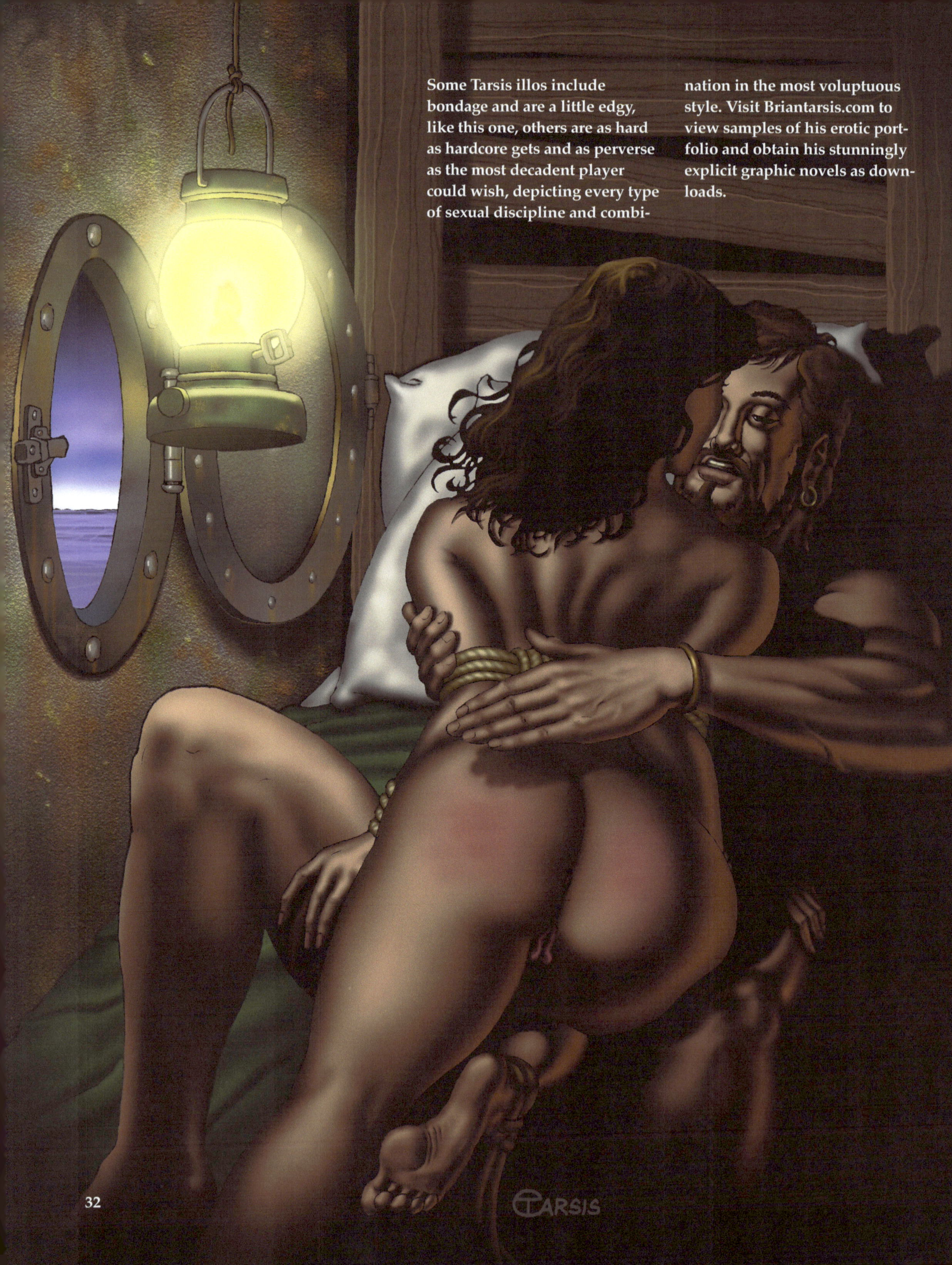

Some Tarsis illos include bondage and are a little edgy, like this one, others are as hard as hardcore gets and as perverse as the most decadent player could wish, depicting every type of sexual discipline and combination in the most voluptuous style. Visit Briantarsis.com to view samples of his erotic portfolio and obtain his stunningly explicit graphic novels as downloads.

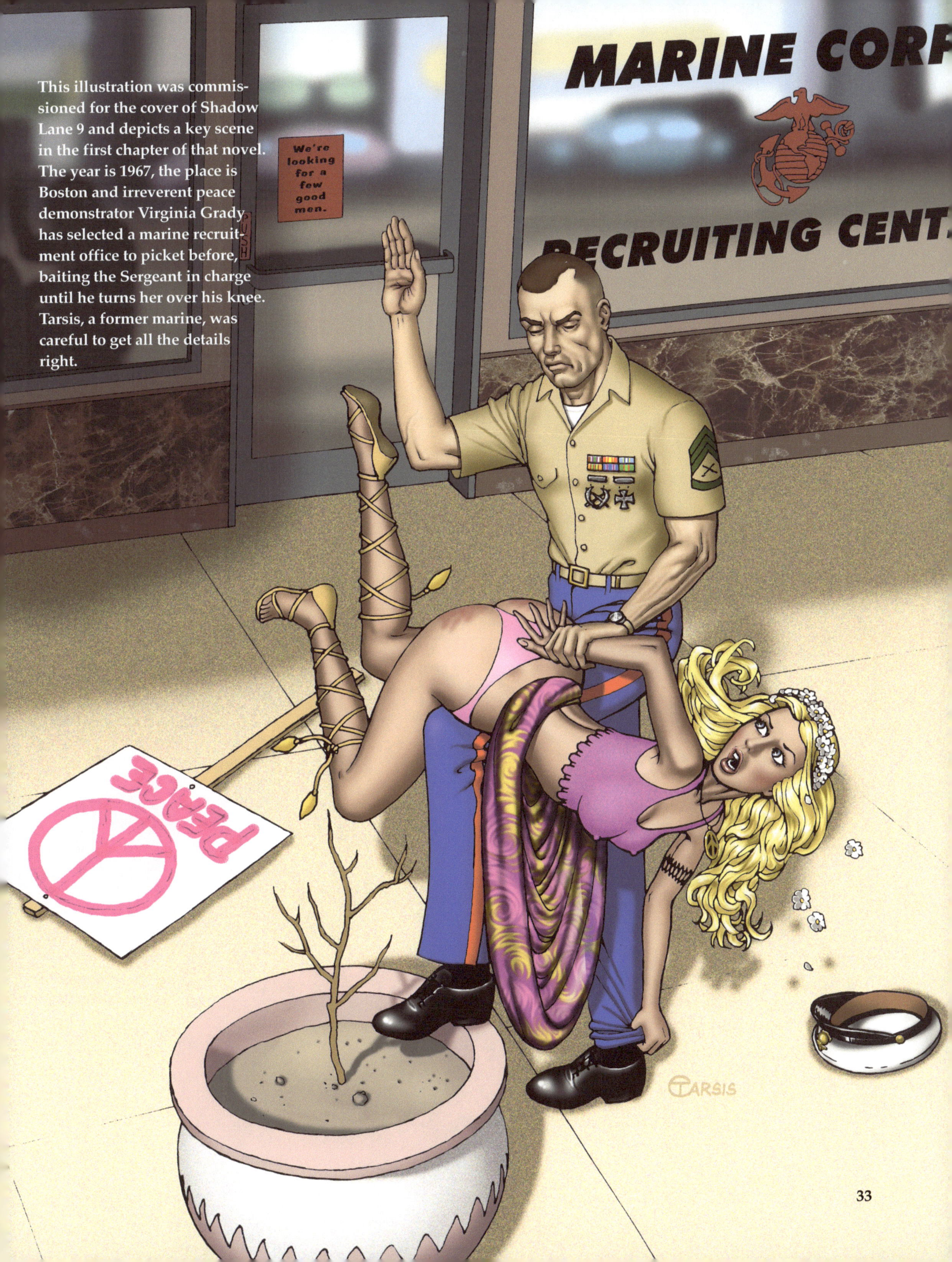

This illustration was commissioned for the cover of Shadow Lane 9 and depicts a key scene in the first chapter of that novel. The year is 1967, the place is Boston and irreverent peace demonstrator Virginia Grady has selected a marine recruitment office to picket before, baiting the Sergeant in charge until he turns her over his knee. Tarsis, a former marine, was careful to get all the details right.

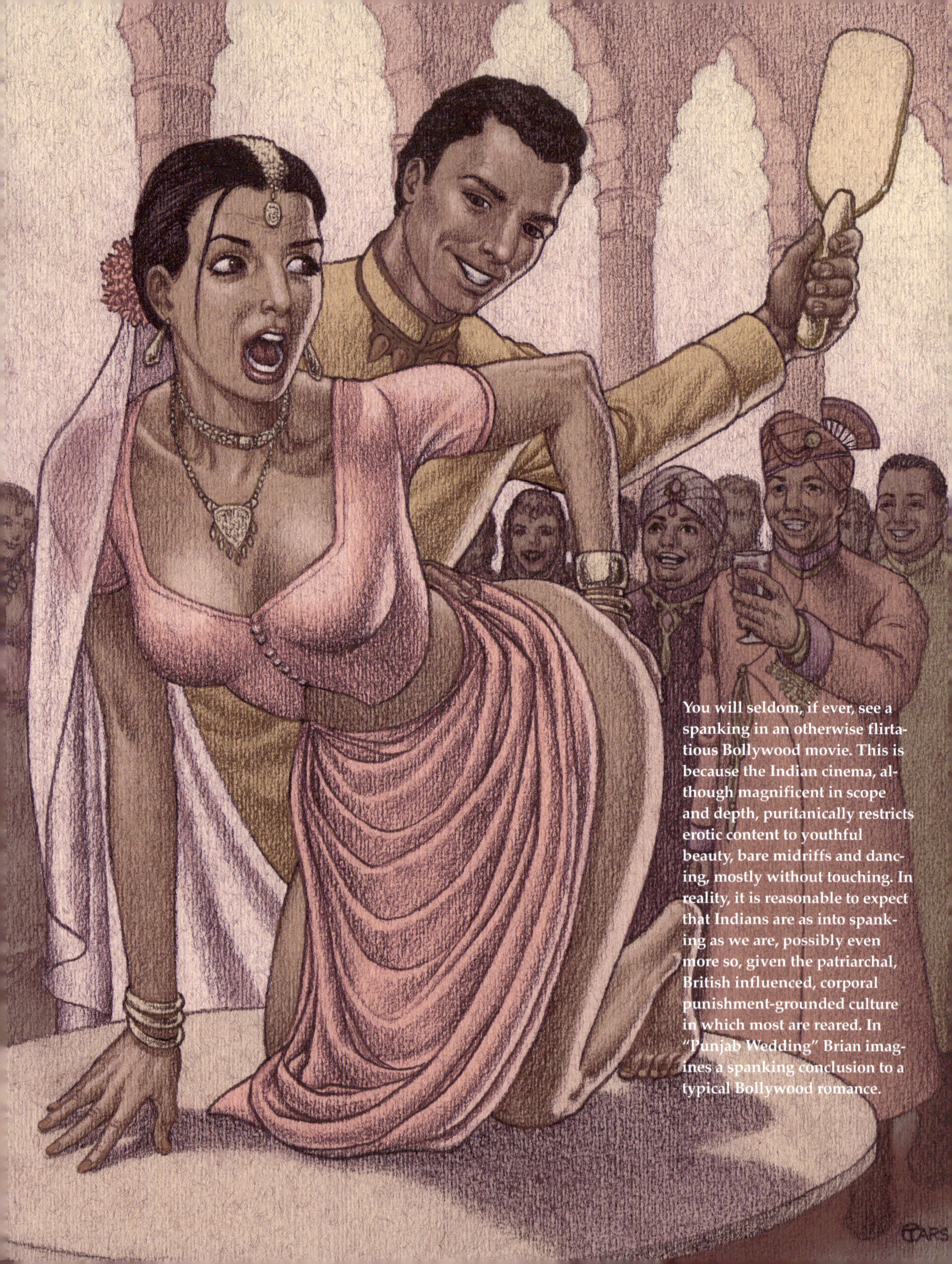

You will seldom, if ever, see a spanking in an otherwise flirtatious Bollywood movie. This is because the Indian cinema, although magnificent in scope and depth, puritanically restricts erotic content to youthful beauty, bare midriffs and dancing, mostly without touching. In reality, it is reasonable to expect that Indians are as into spanking as we are, possibly even more so, given the patriarchal, British influenced, corporal punishment-grounded culture in which most are reared. In "Punjab Wedding" Brian imagines a spanking conclusion to a typical Bollywood romance.

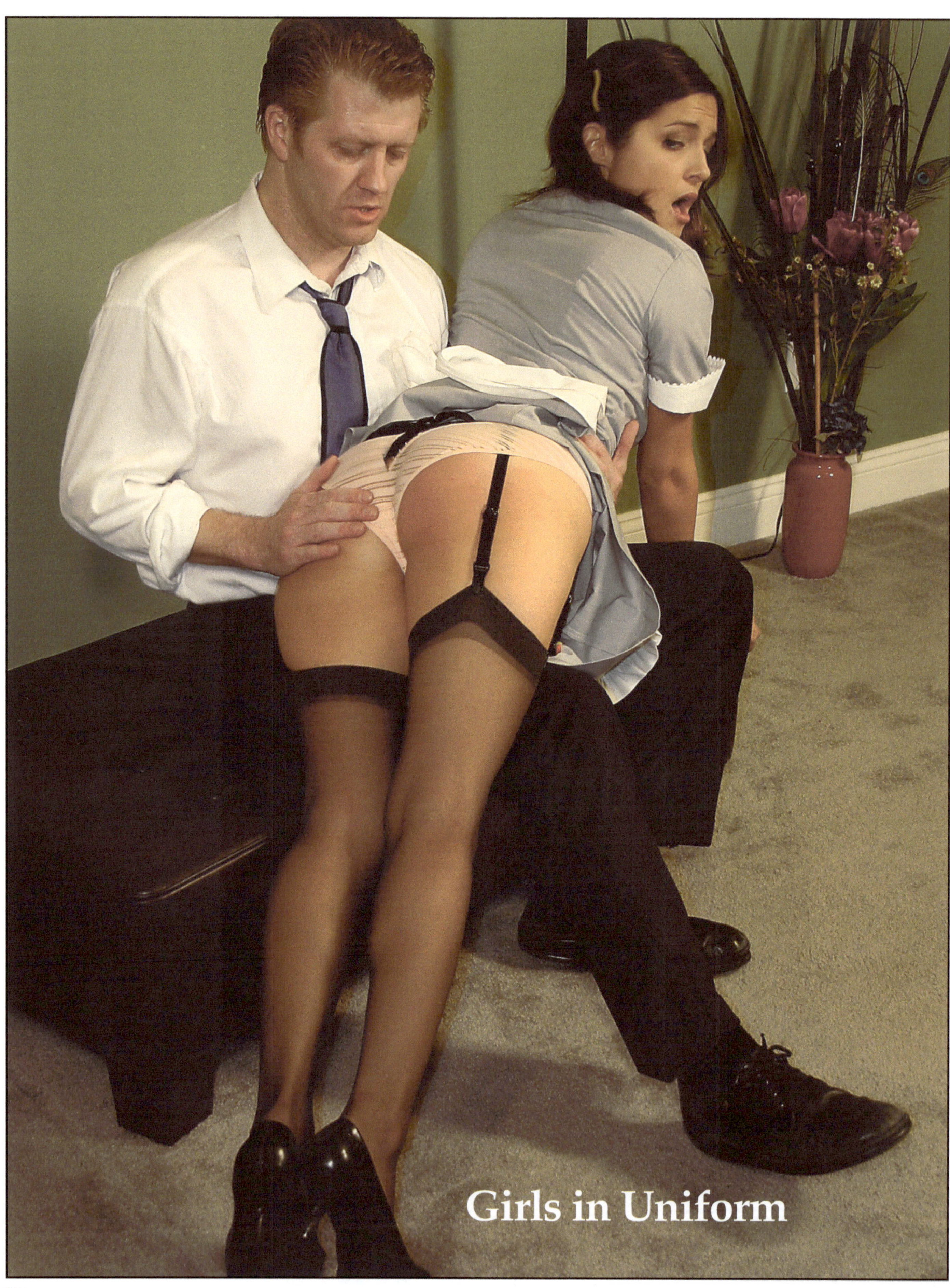
Girls in Uniform

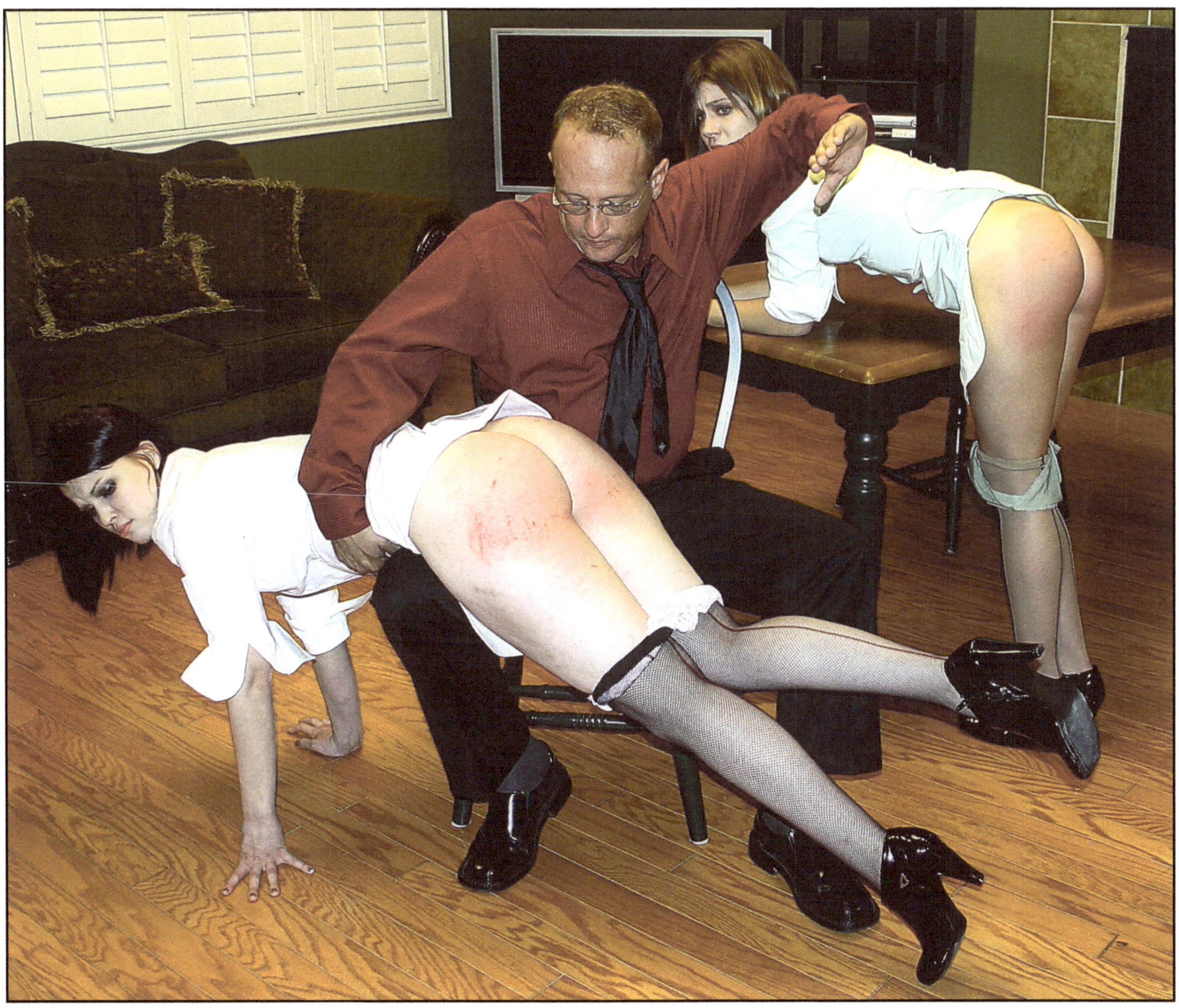

Opposite page
Any girl who is seriously into spanking will possess some sort of fetish wardrobe, be it ever so basic as a black garter belt, sheer stockings and heels. But your alpha submissives and spoiled rotten brats are apt to take the fantasy many steps further by providing themselves with smart costumes to suit every fantasy. While Samantha appears on our cover in her formal maid's outfit, of black satin over yards of white nylon petticoat, she is spanked here in a much more severe daytime maid's uniform, complete with starched white apron. Women who enjoy being spanked dress for their spankings and the men who are administering them. The black velvet bow atop her sheer, peach, full-seated briefs has the effect of presenting Samantha's perfect bottom in the form of a present to be unwrapped. In this case the naughty housemaid's exacting employer is portrayed by Danny Chrighton in the video "At Your Service".

Above
In this scene from "Authority Figure" Kailee and Abigail Whittaker play irresponsible au pair girls who infuriate their employer with extreme misbehavior. The stunning brats know they are on the verge of being fired and so submit to discipline from Lance del Toro, who portrays the exasperated householder. Abigail is from the Midwest, Kailee from the Rockies and Lance from Arizona. He's old enough to be their dad and spanks like some mythical dad from the 1950's, hard enough to make the sting last.

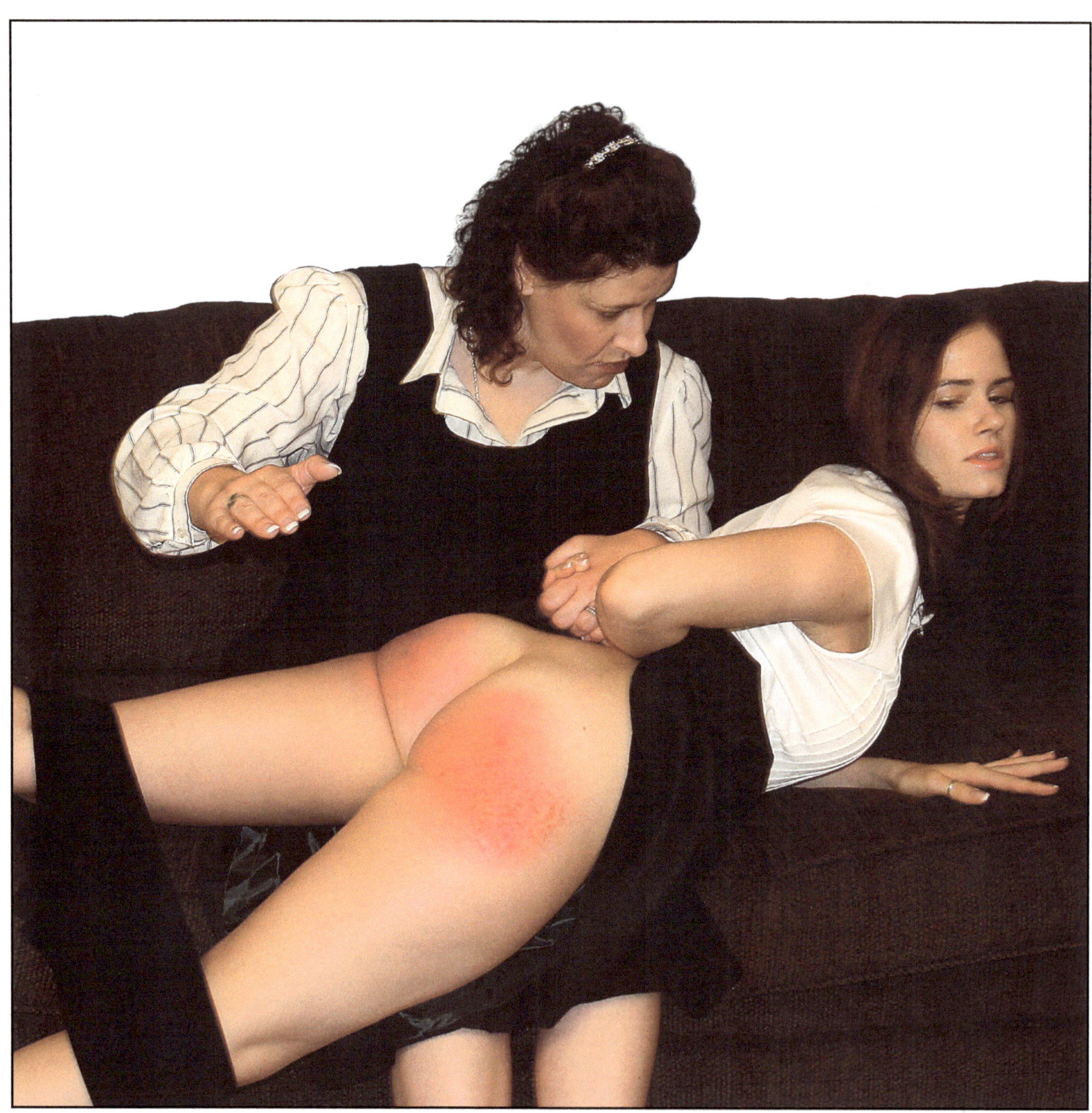

Braemar Academy is a fantasy location we've returned to again and again in our books and videos for more than twenty years. It is populated by teachers who spank, spankable teachers and spoiled rotten preppies in crisp white shirts and pleated skirts. Headmistress this semester is Miss Chris, shown here administering a traditional, over the knee, bare bottom spanking to her impertinent pupil Jenni Mack.

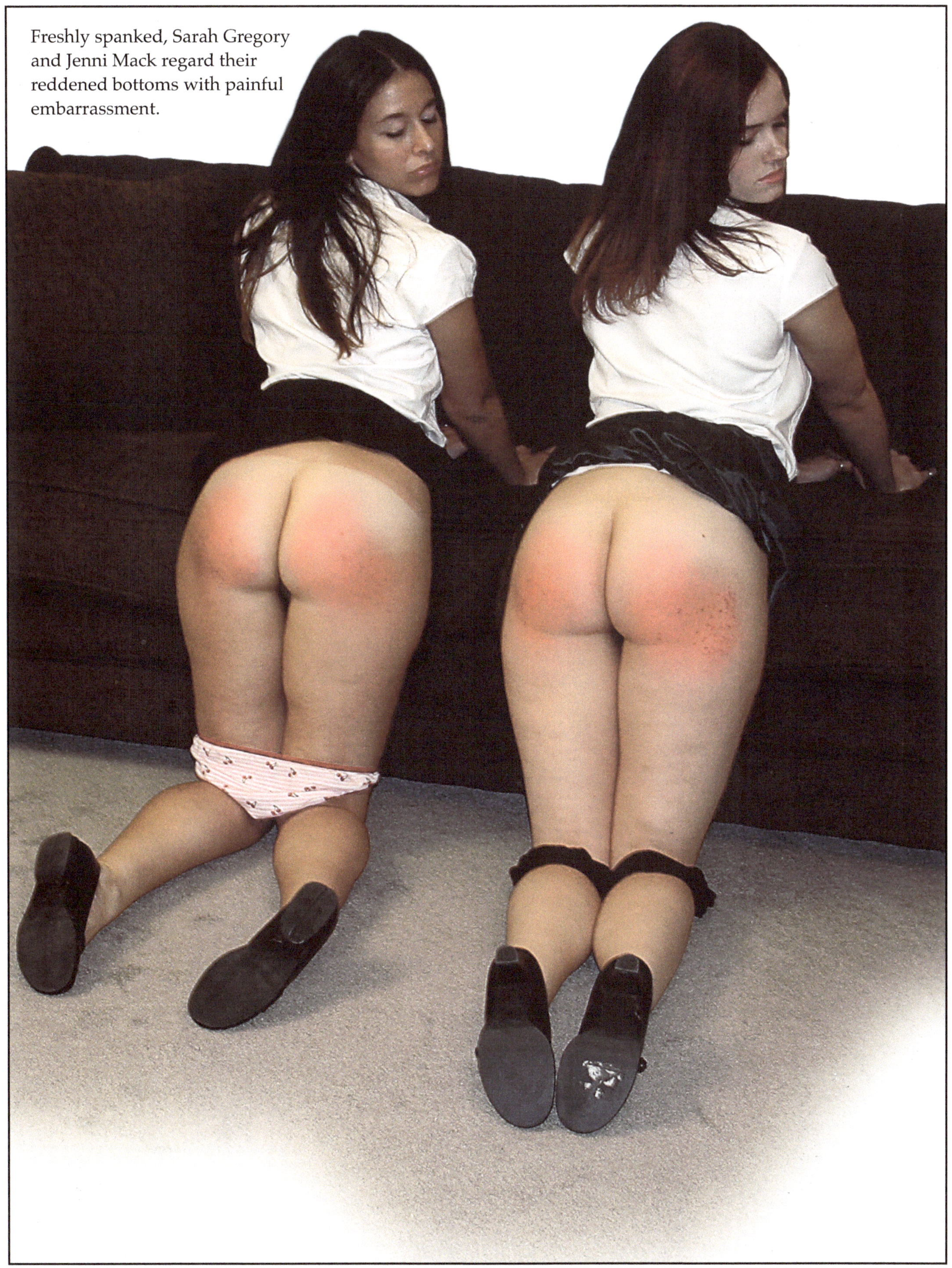
Freshly spanked, Sarah Gregory and Jenni Mack regard their reddened bottoms with painful embarrassment.

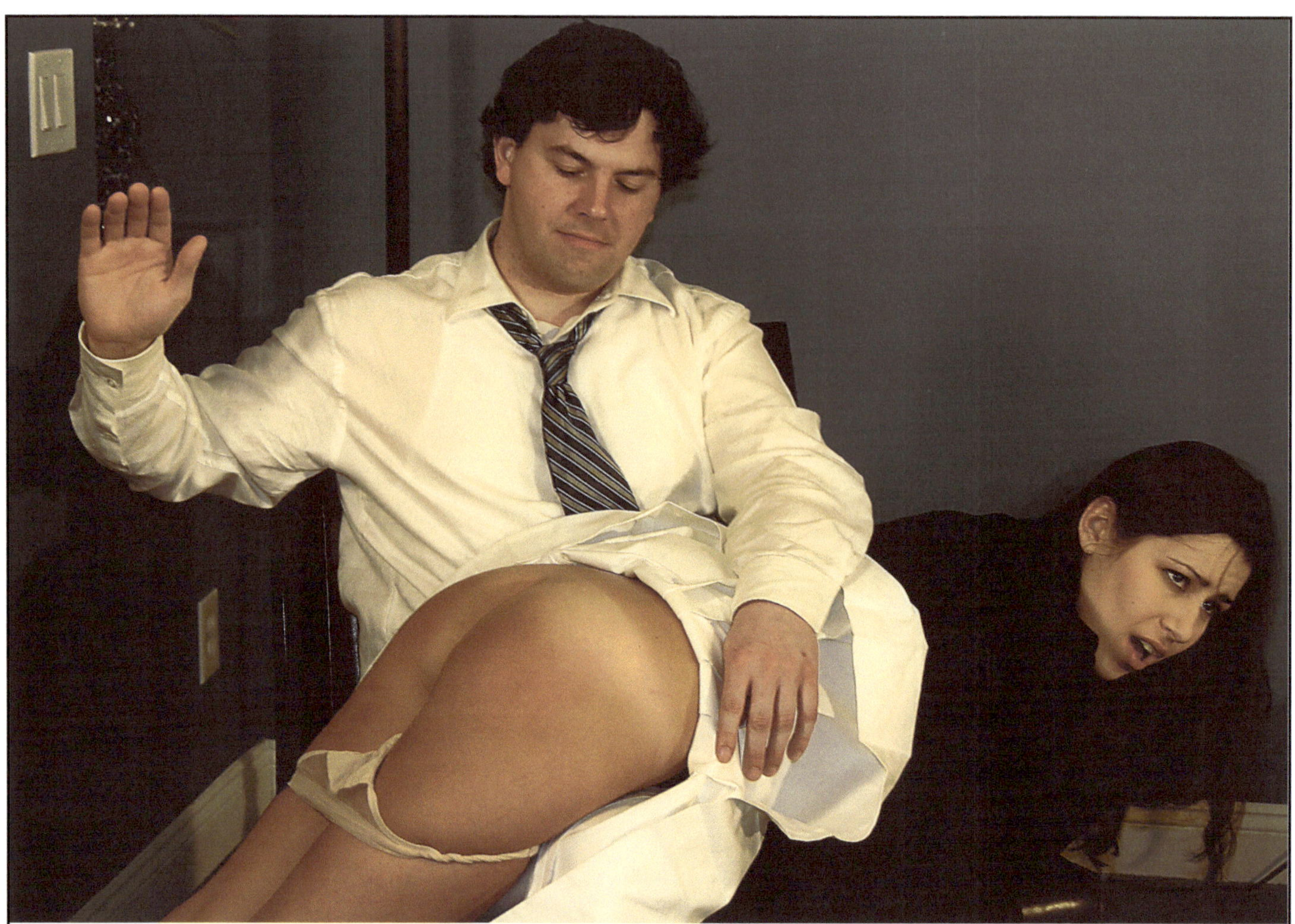

Sierra Salem

Wild Beauty

Sierra Salem burst onto the scene when she was only eighteen. With her glowing natural beauty, modest bashfulness and innate enthusiasm for spanking, she knocked everyone out. Sierra fits into a preppie fantasy as though it were made for her. With her long, dark, silky hair, large, expressive eyes and wide, arresting mouth, not to mention that trim but delightfully well rounded bottom, set off to advantage by those sexy tan lines, Sierra simply looks like the kind pampered brat who really should be spanked. Here she is administered to by Mike Nous in a scene from "Heirs to Misfortune".

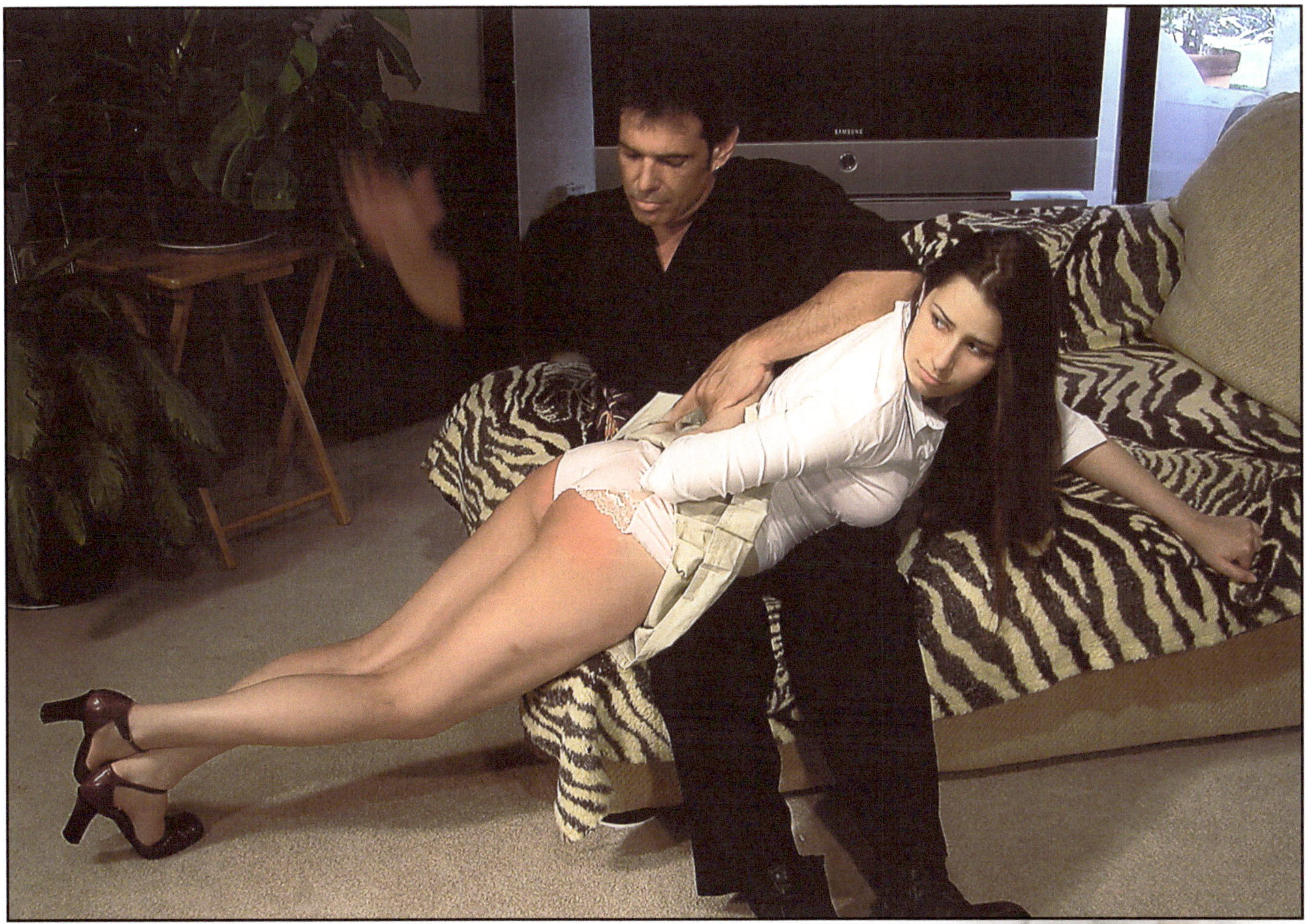

One thing Sierra wasn't shy about was her attraction to veteran disciplinarian Dallas, as can be seen in her womanly body language and provocative expression in this scene from "To Have and to Scold". Sierra was nineteen, lovely and not above trying to wheedle and whine her way out of a hard spanking.

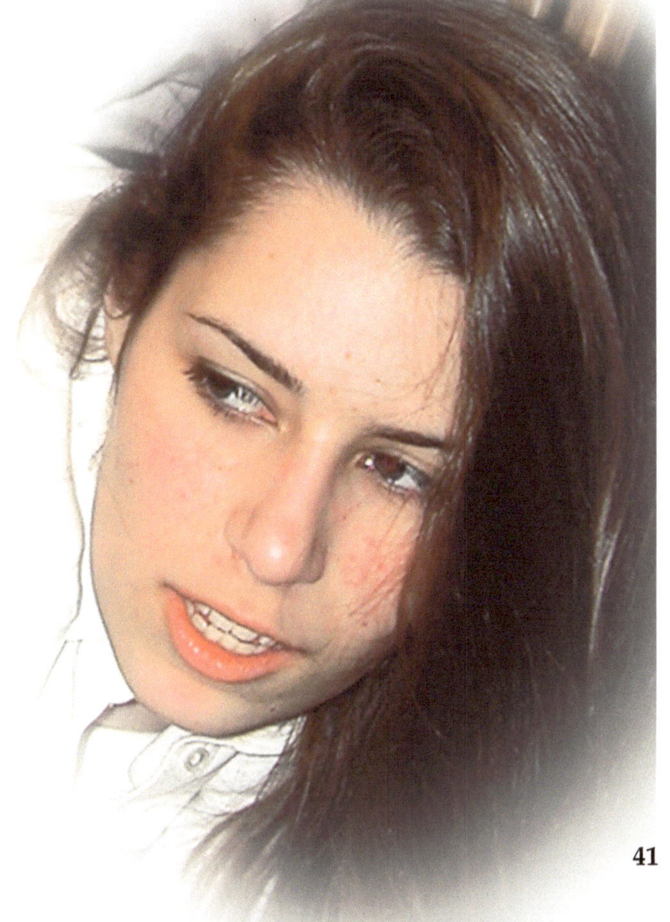

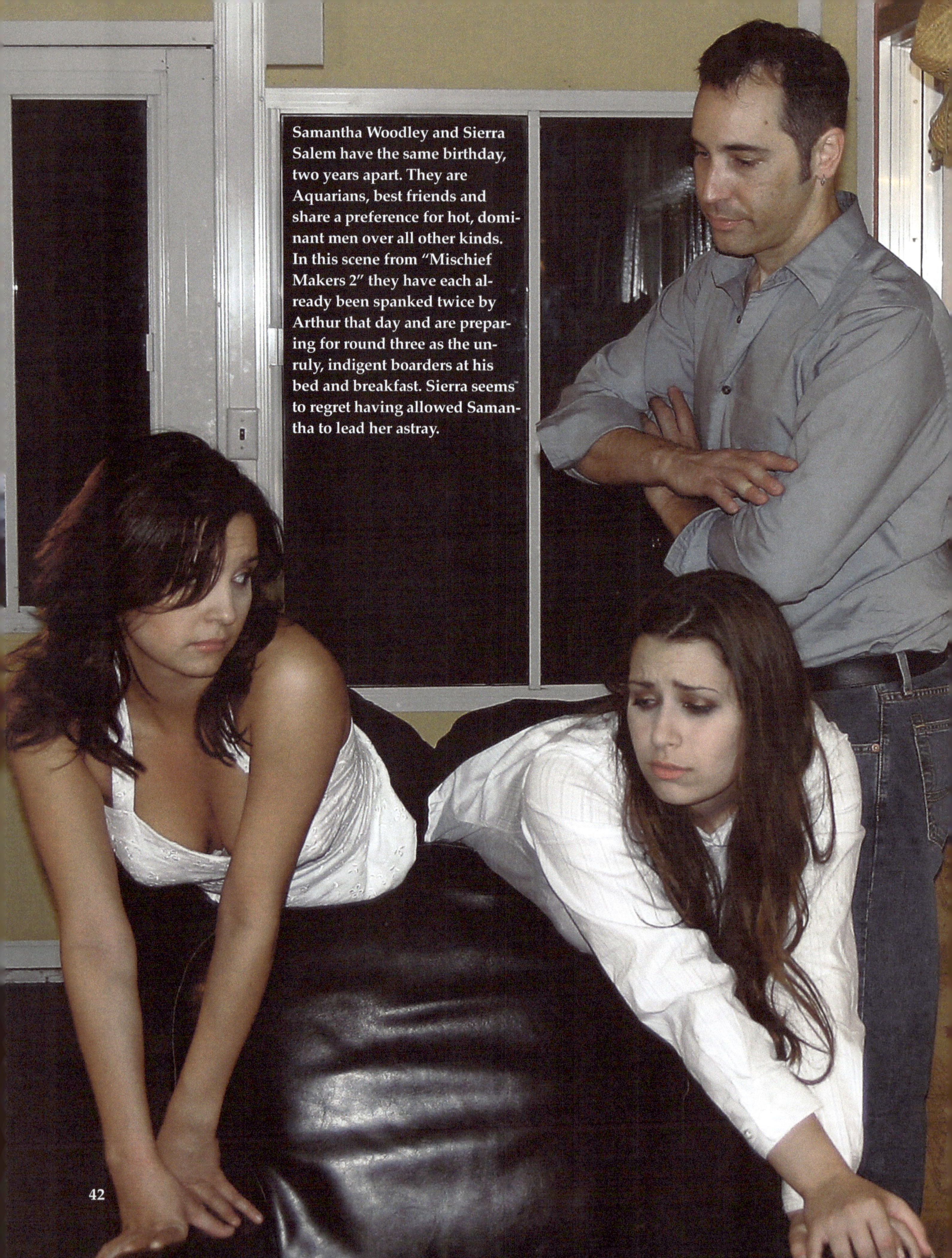

Samantha Woodley and Sierra Salem have the same birthday, two years apart. They are Aquarians, best friends and share a preference for hot, dominant men over all other kinds. In this scene from "Mischief Makers 2" they have each already been spanked twice by Arthur that day and are preparing for round three as the unruly, indigent boarders at his bed and breakfast. Sierra seems to regret having allowed Samantha to lead her astray.

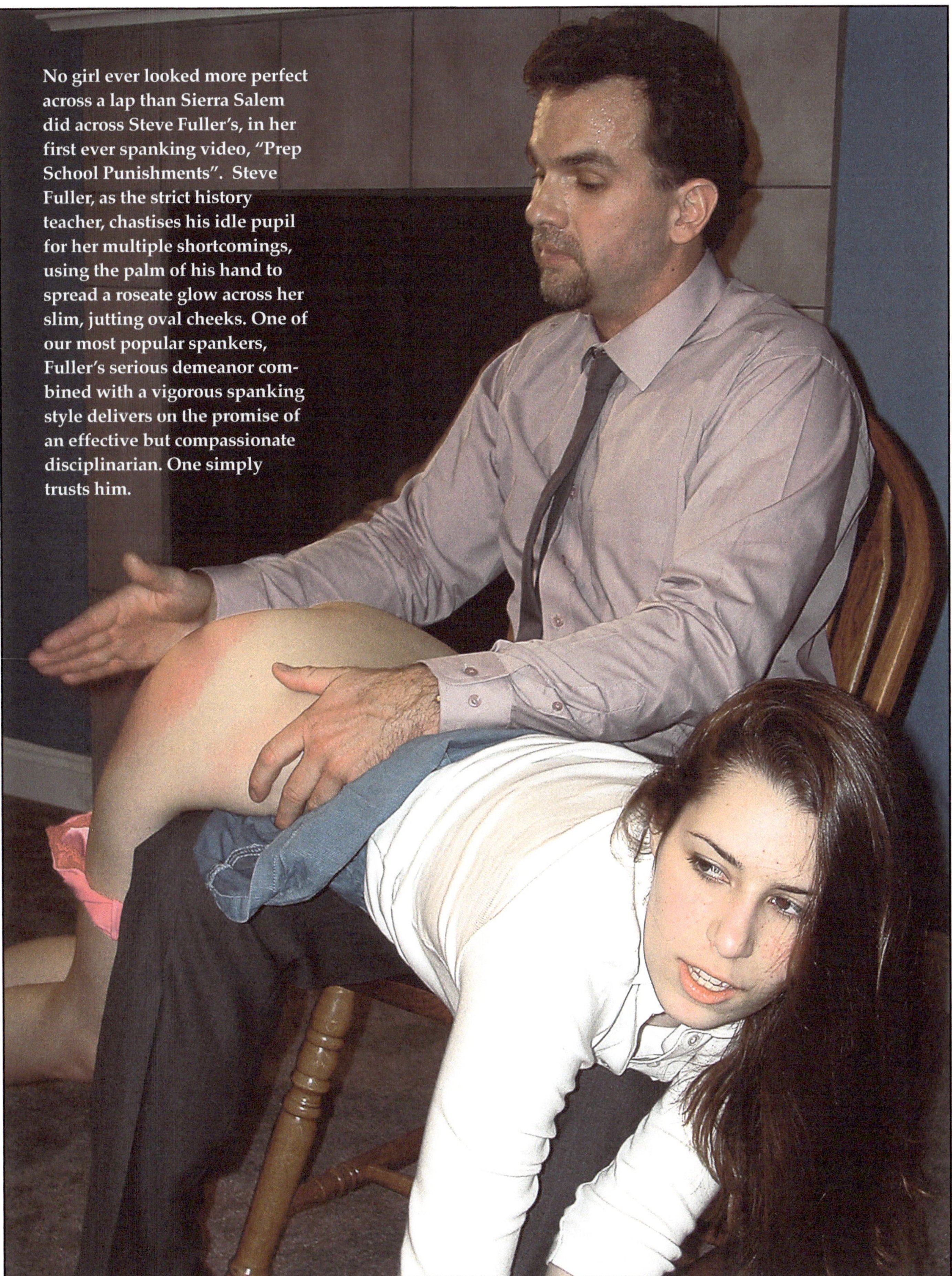

No girl ever looked more perfect across a lap than Sierra Salem did across Steve Fuller's, in her first ever spanking video, "Prep School Punishments". Steve Fuller, as the strict history teacher, chastises his idle pupil for her multiple shortcomings, using the palm of his hand to spread a roseate glow across her slim, jutting oval cheeks. One of our most popular spankers, Fuller's serious demeanor combined with a vigorous spanking style delivers on the promise of an effective but compassionate disciplinarian. One simply trusts him.

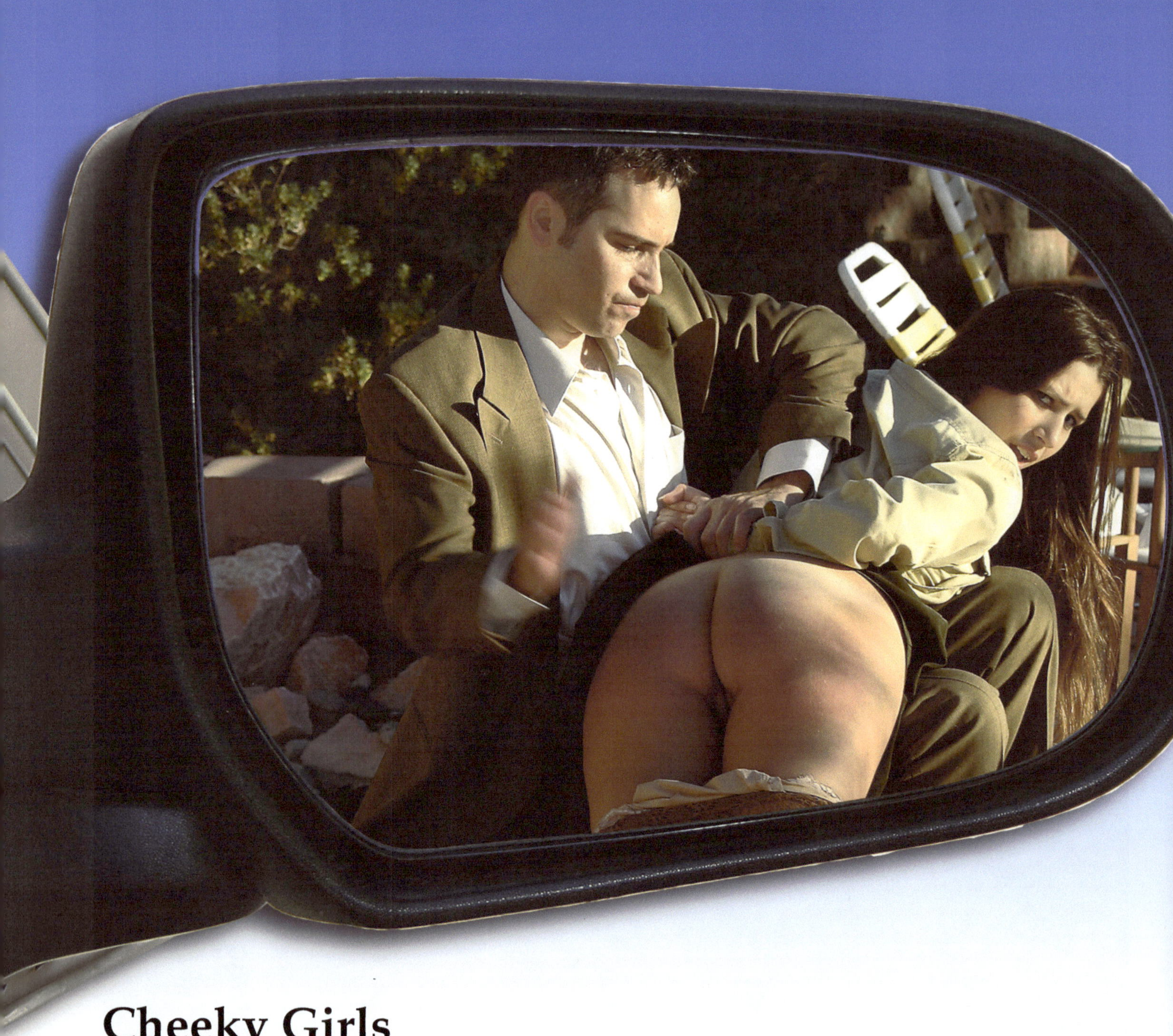

Cheeky Girls

Views of the Rear

Textured tights and creamy briefs pulled down to half-mast display Sierra Salem's perfect bottom charmingly. Preppie brats dressed like this in the 60's, with their long, straight hair luxuriantly hanging down.

Opposite page
Most spanking fans agree that one of the prettiest and most provocative sights in the world is that of a shapely female bottom, up-turned and freshly pink from a good spanking.

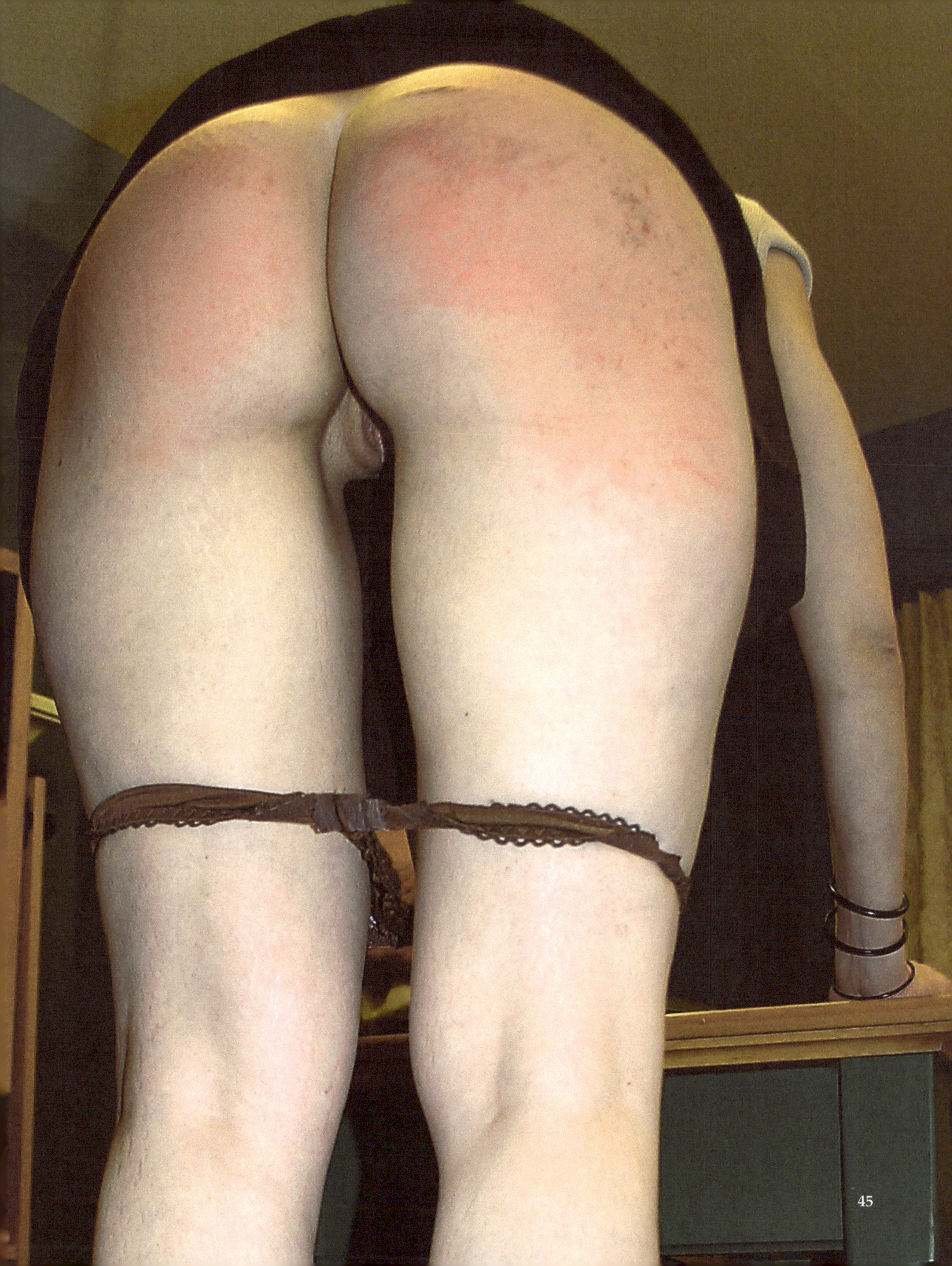

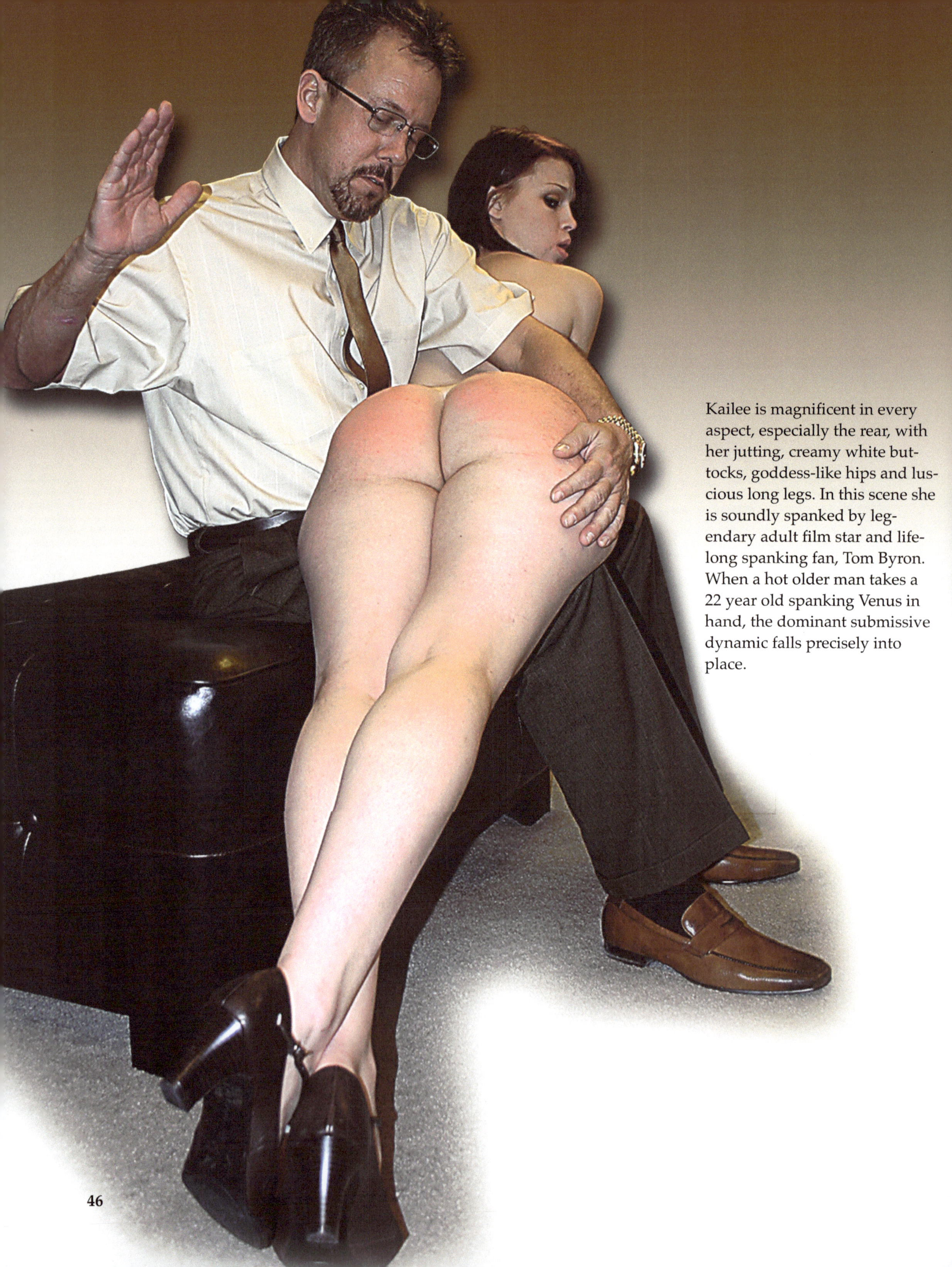

Kailee is magnificent in every aspect, especially the rear, with her jutting, creamy white buttocks, goddess-like hips and luscious long legs. In this scene she is soundly spanked by legendary adult film star and lifelong spanking fan, Tom Byron. When a hot older man takes a 22 year old spanking Venus in hand, the dominant submissive dynamic falls precisely into place.

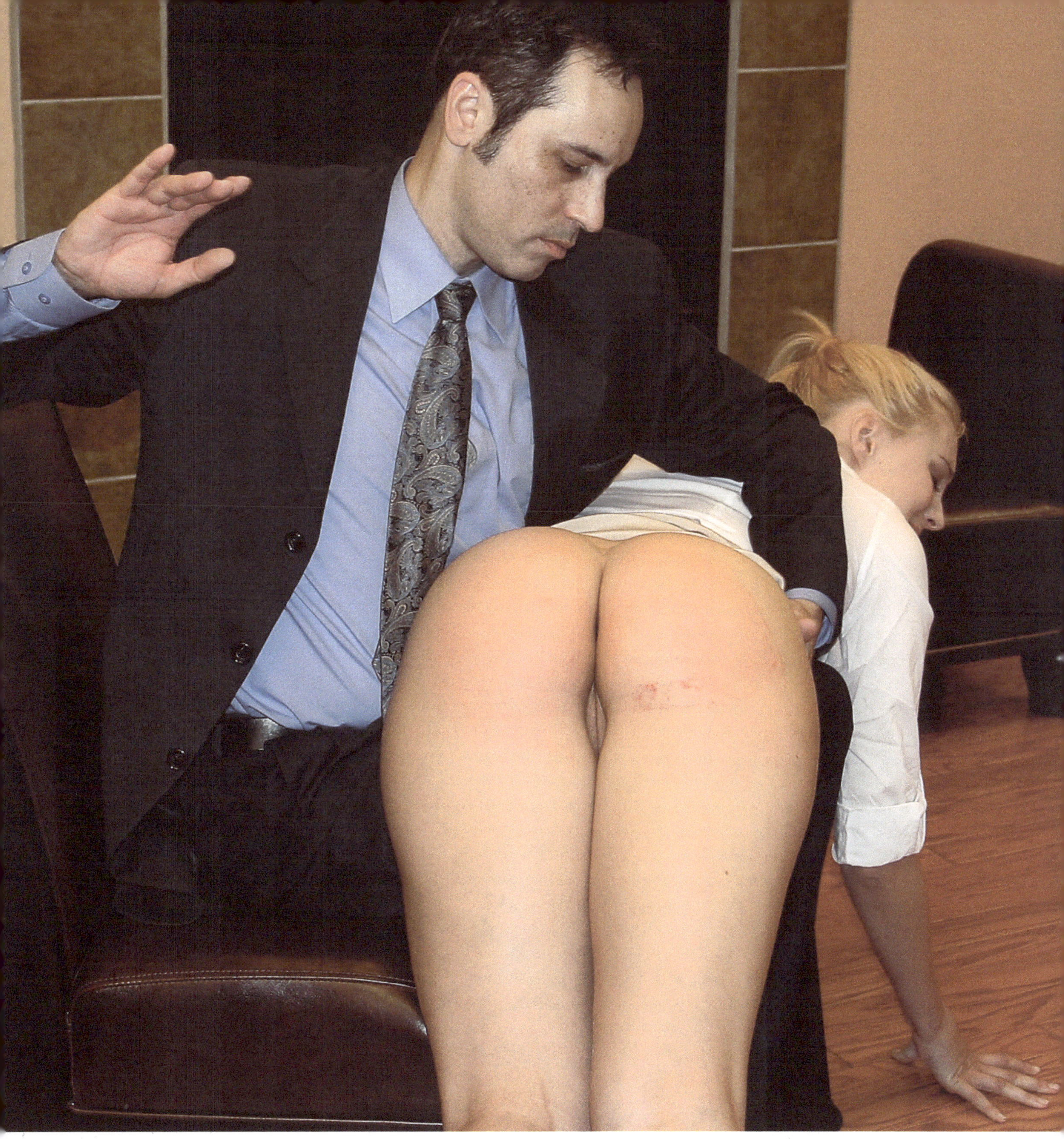

With her slender buttocks, so daintily rounded and invitingly upthrust and her long, well muscled, dancer's legs tautly stretched, Amelia Rutherford presents a picture of elegant vulnerability.

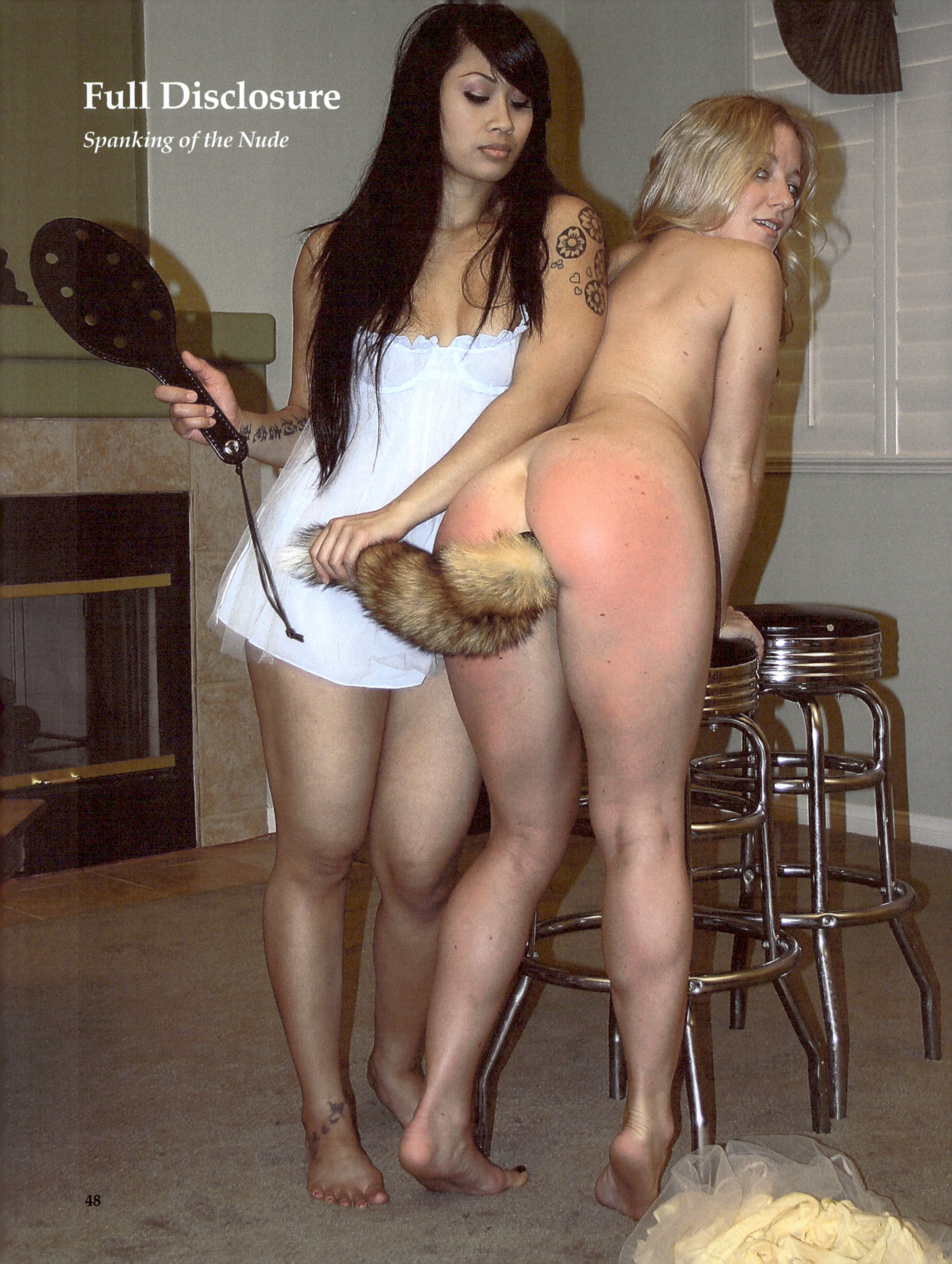

Full Disclosure

Spanking of the Nude

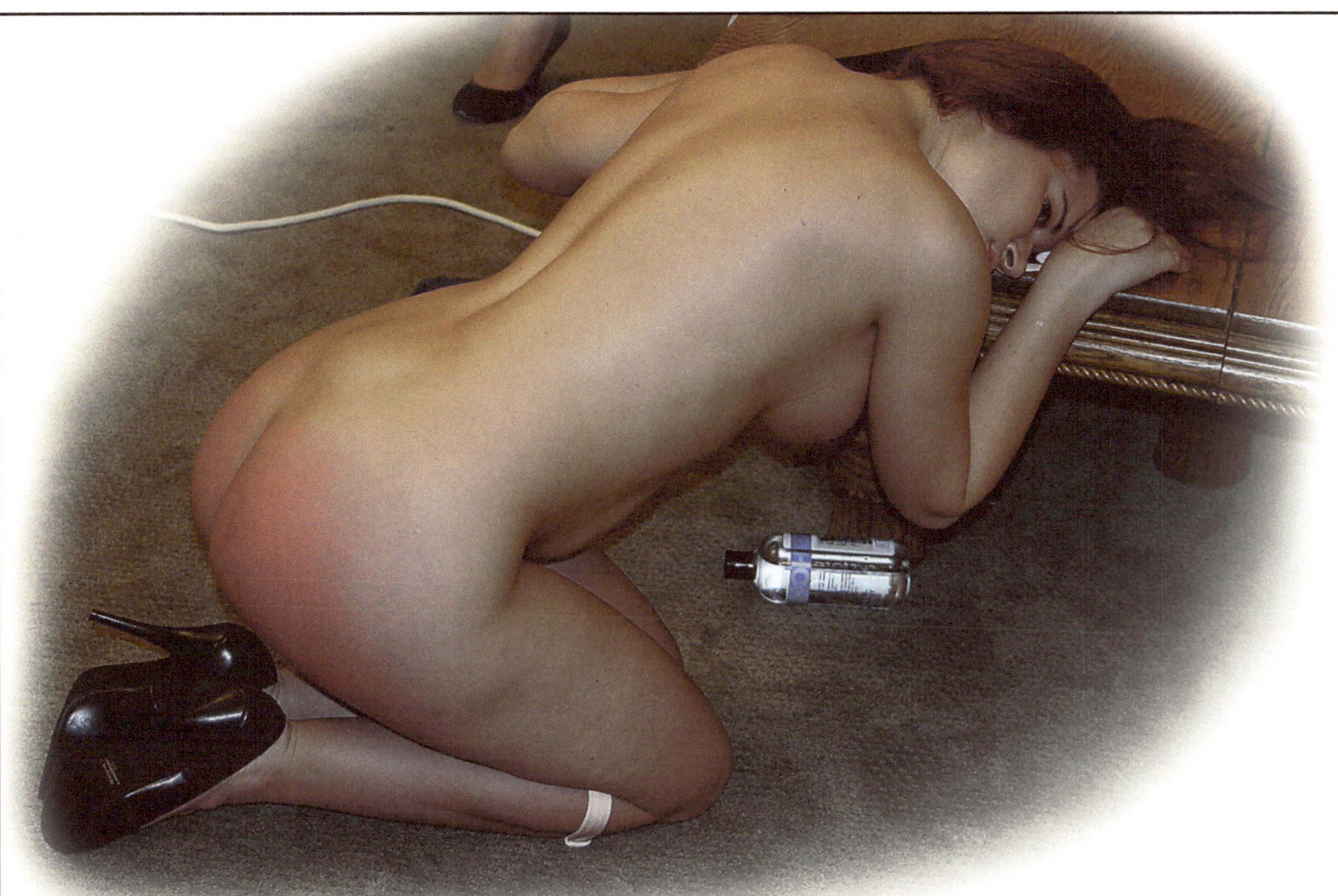

Opposite

When a girl into spanking gets nude to play, she will sometimes agree to go further. Spankees as crazy into it as Dia Zerva describe a wild endorphin rush accompanying the best type of scene that actually stimulates a desire to indulge in even naughtier erotic behavior. Spank such a submissive into a frenzy of pleasure and there's a good chance you'll be invited to take her however you can. Here Lily has chosen a furry tailed buttplug to complete the mastery of her soundly paddled playmate.The scene is from an explicit all-woman video called "Babydoll Bottoms", wherein the girls play pledges to the Lambda Sigma Zeta sorority, another Shadow Lane institution that has been operational for the last twenty years via our Our Sorority series.

Above

Every picture tells a story and this one features unmistakable clues to the erotic activities which preceded the exact moment it was snapped. In "Babydoll Bottoms" the devious and manipulative sorority sister Sarah Blake has just been disciplined and completely undone by the savvy pledges she has had the audacity to bedevil earlier on. The spanking she has received is evident through her deeply colored buttocks; the dildo penetration she has been submitted to is implied through the presence of the bottle of lube and a powerful vibrator wand cast aside gives testament to the orgasm she has been forced to give up to her demanding sorority sisters in the course of her punishment. Sarah kneels with her rosy bottom uppermost and her toys scattered around her as her spasms of embarrassed excitement ebb away.

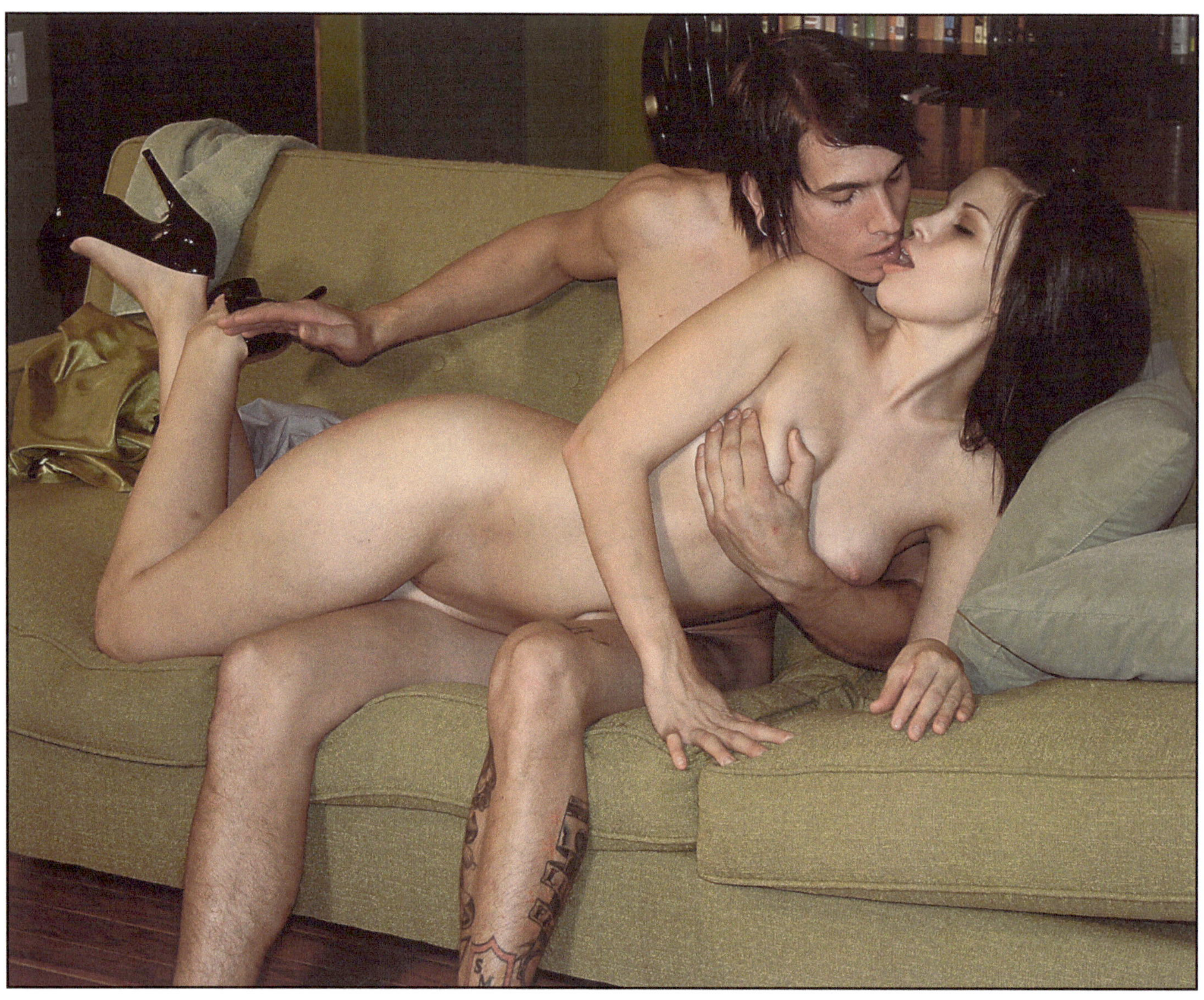

Kailee wanted to do her first sex and spanking video for Shadow Lane and brought along a hot boy she was dating named Seth to add verisimilitude to the production. Spanking is the primary form of foreplay for every true spanking enthusiast, which doesn't mean that we can't enjoy intercourse for its own sake, but only that it is much hotter when preceded by an excellent corporal punishment interlude with a compatible partner with whom we have perfect chemistry.

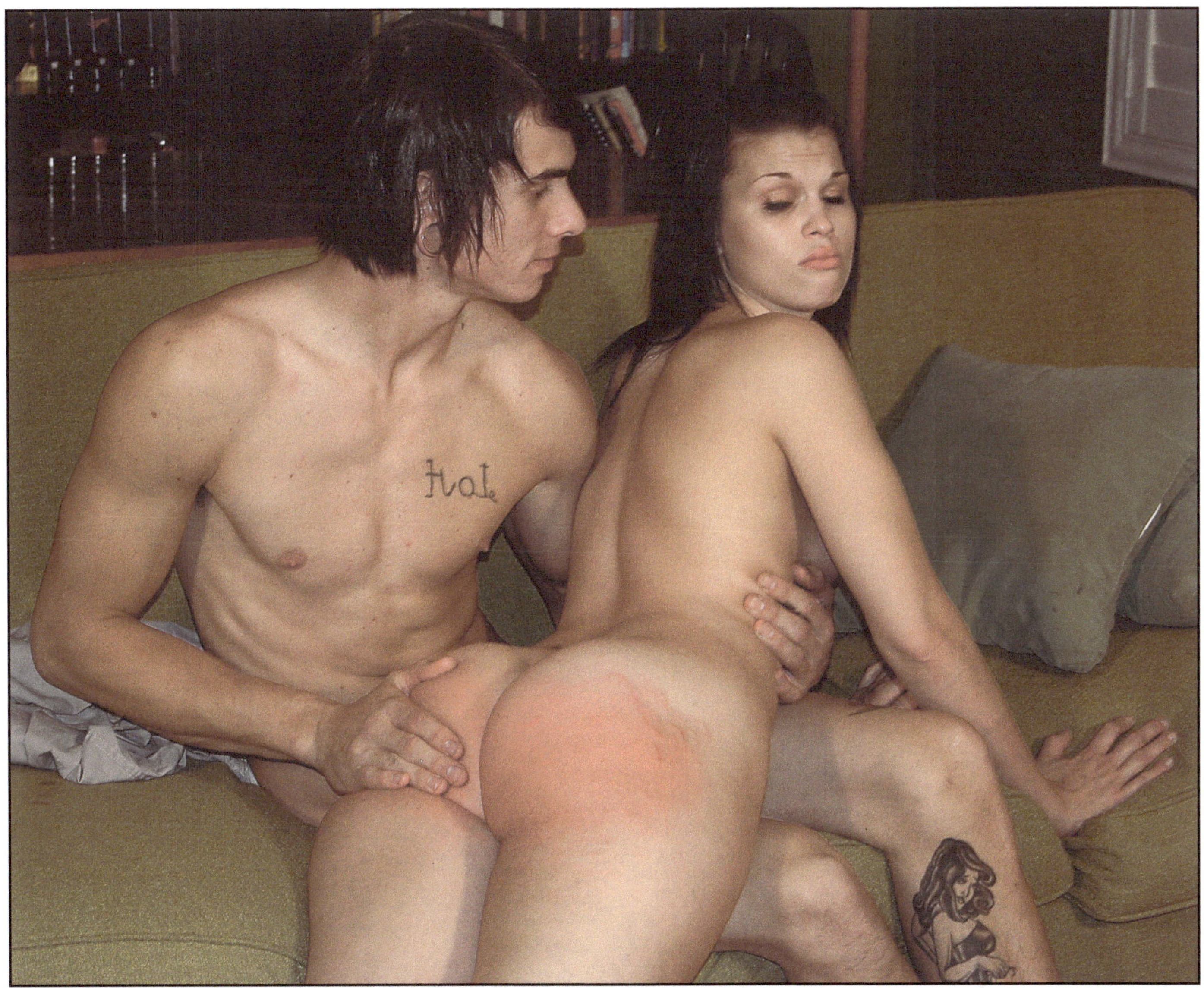

You don't have to dress in suits and ties or perfect town and country outfits or be born in the 1950's to believe in and practice the romance of discipline. The fact that the dynamic B&D subculture appeals to the hippest and the youngest among us should surprise no one. Kids of the 21st century love going to demonstrable extremes and corporal punishment fits into that lifestyle like a tiny waist fits into a corset.

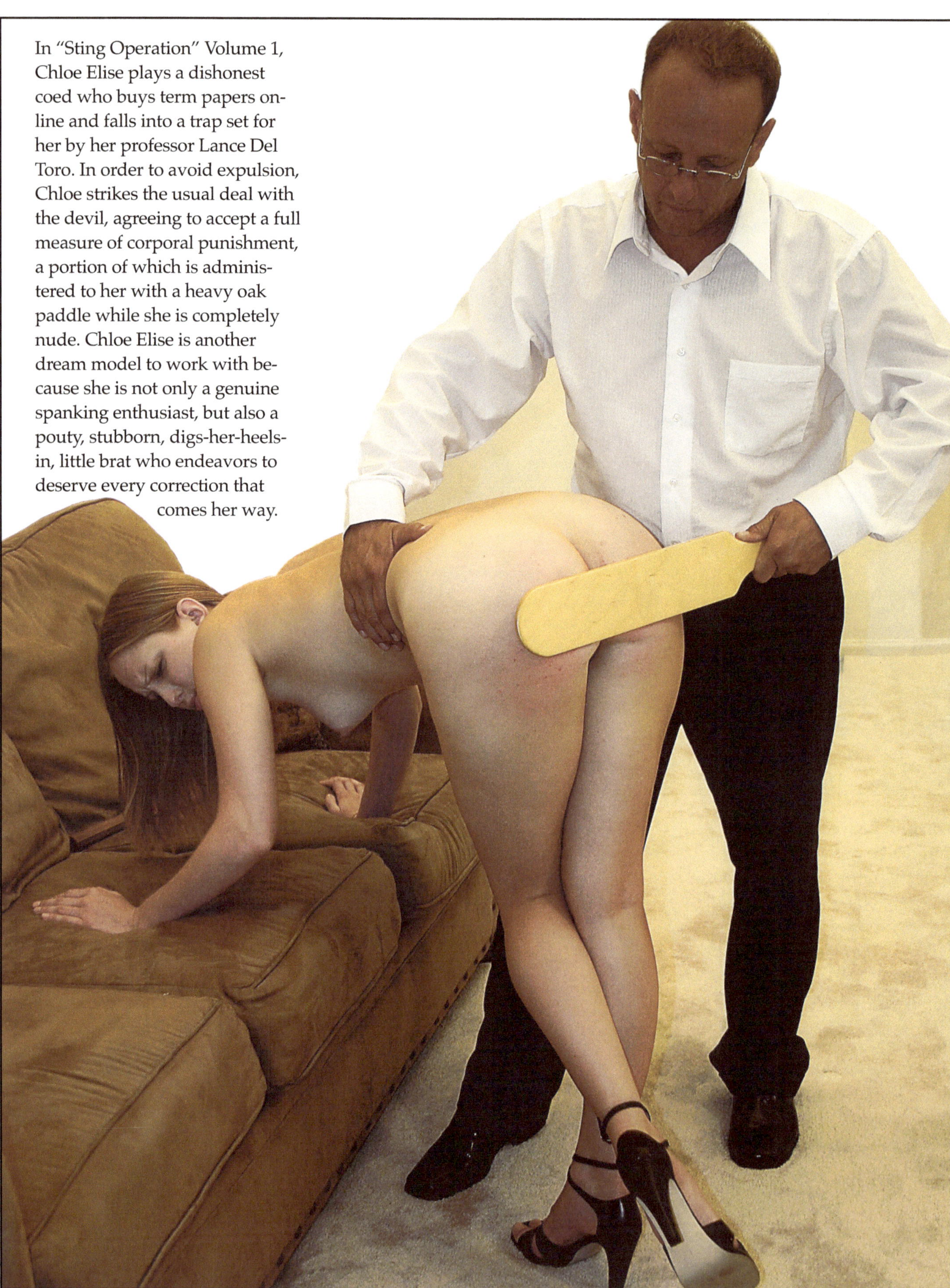

In "Sting Operation" Volume 1, Chloe Elise plays a dishonest coed who buys term papers online and falls into a trap set for her by her professor Lance Del Toro. In order to avoid expulsion, Chloe strikes the usual deal with the devil, agreeing to accept a full measure of corporal punishment, a portion of which is administered to her with a heavy oak paddle while she is completely nude. Chloe Elise is another dream model to work with because she is not only a genuine spanking enthusiast, but also a pouty, stubborn, digs-her-heels-in, little brat who endeavors to deserve every correction that comes her way.

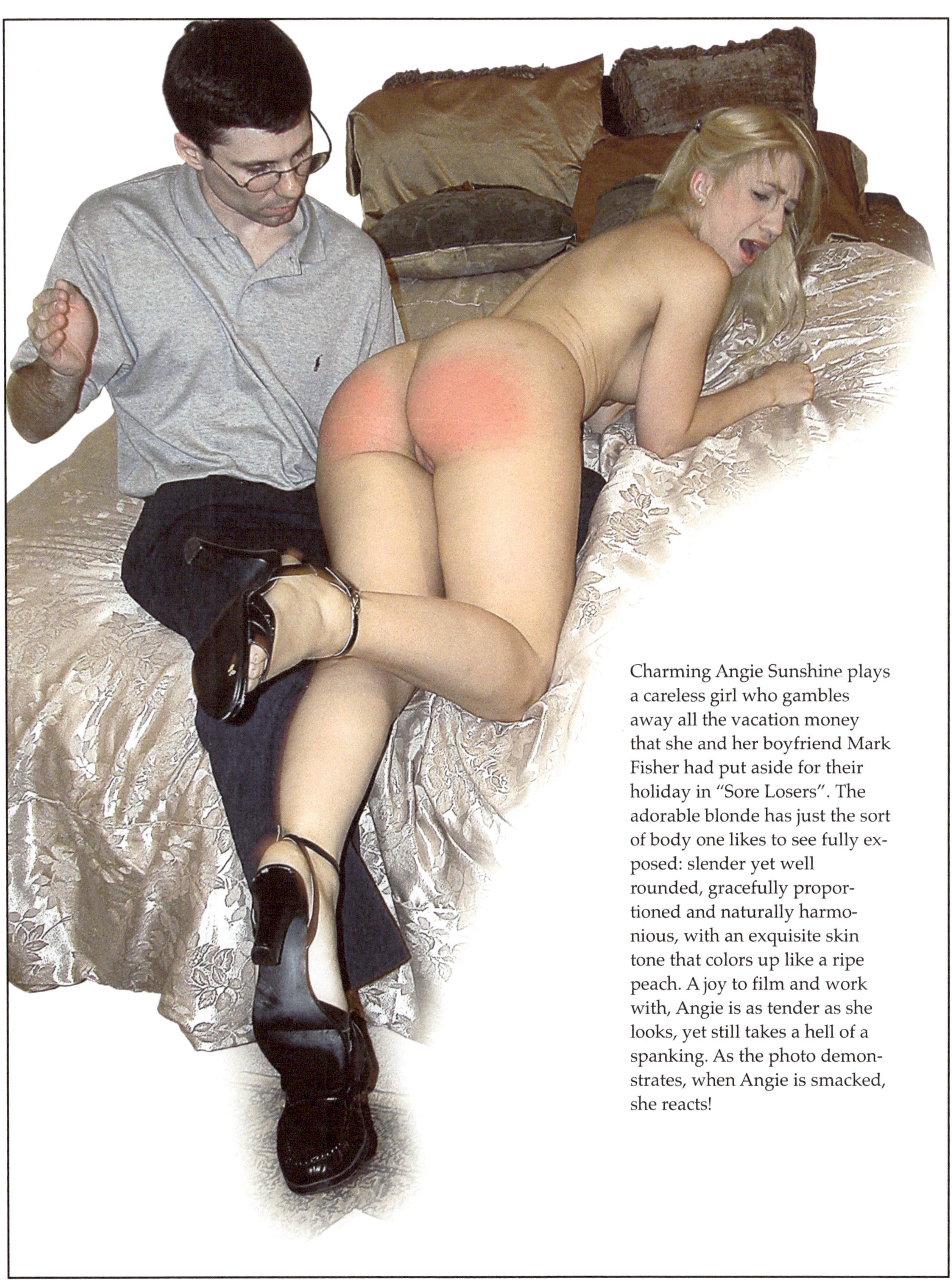

Charming Angie Sunshine plays a careless girl who gambles away all the vacation money that she and her boyfriend Mark Fisher had put aside for their holiday in "Sore Losers". The adorable blonde has just the sort of body one likes to see fully exposed: slender yet well rounded, gracefully proportioned and naturally harmonious, with an exquisite skin tone that colors up like a ripe peach. A joy to film and work with, Angie is as tender as she looks, yet still takes a hell of a spanking. As the photo demonstrates, when Angie is smacked, she reacts!

Clinical Study

The Anal Erotic Obsession

Featuring
Dia Zerva *as the patient*
Larry Selden *as the doctor*
Chelsea Pfeiffer *as the nurse*

Dressing as though it were still the mid-20th century is highly appropriate for a spanking session, providing not only a modicum of modesty, but several layers of fine cloth to unpeel, prior to the inevitable revelation of bare, pink skin. But within a multi-textural spanking scene, a girl may begin buttoned down and end up completely undone.

Have you noticed that the most ladylike girls often entertain the most extreme fantasies? The invasive spanking and enema therapy session in the privacy of the exclusive clinic is a submissive daydream shared by every anally oriented girl who is also into spanking.

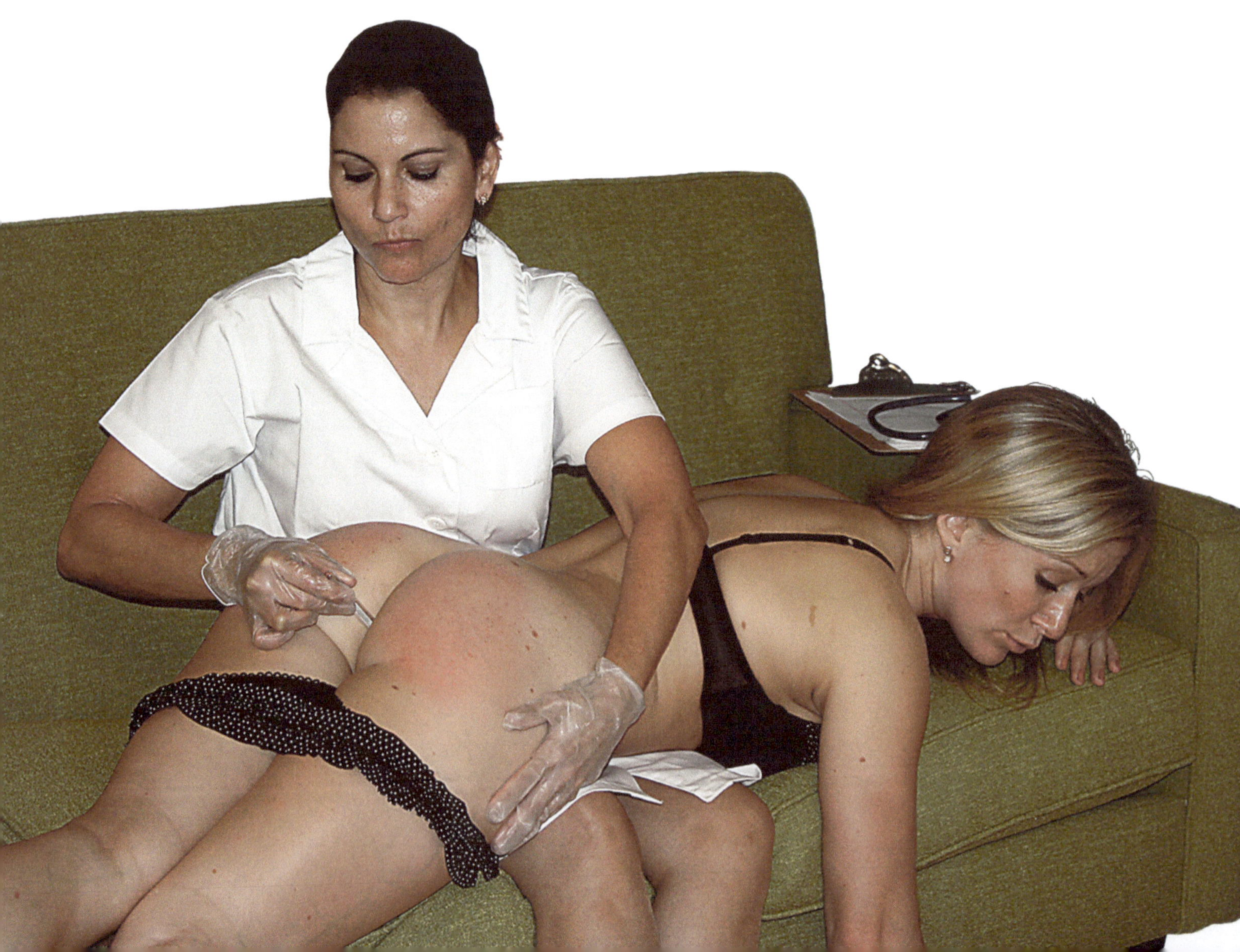

Rectal temperature taking is part of the ritual. The sensation of being attended to is seductive and the procedure itself exquisitely arousing, and yet it is also important to stress that this is discipline therapy. That is why the accompanying spanking is always fairly hard.

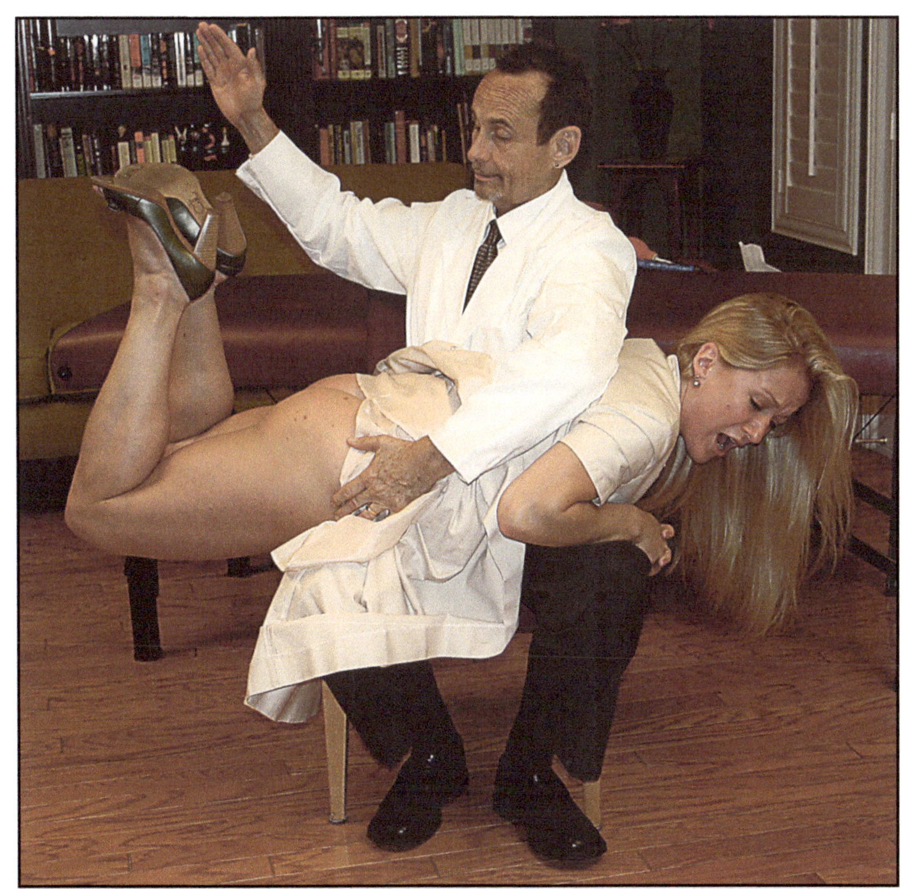

In this session, Dr. Selden administers a series of syringe enemas using a colorful boxed set of bulb douches, each nozzle with a slightly different shape. A vast array of colonic cleansing devices are available as hygienic sex toys online, and many enthusiasts find this a much more comfortable way of shopping for such items than in person. These scenes are from "The Doctor Is In" an explicit Shadow Lane spanking and enema video.

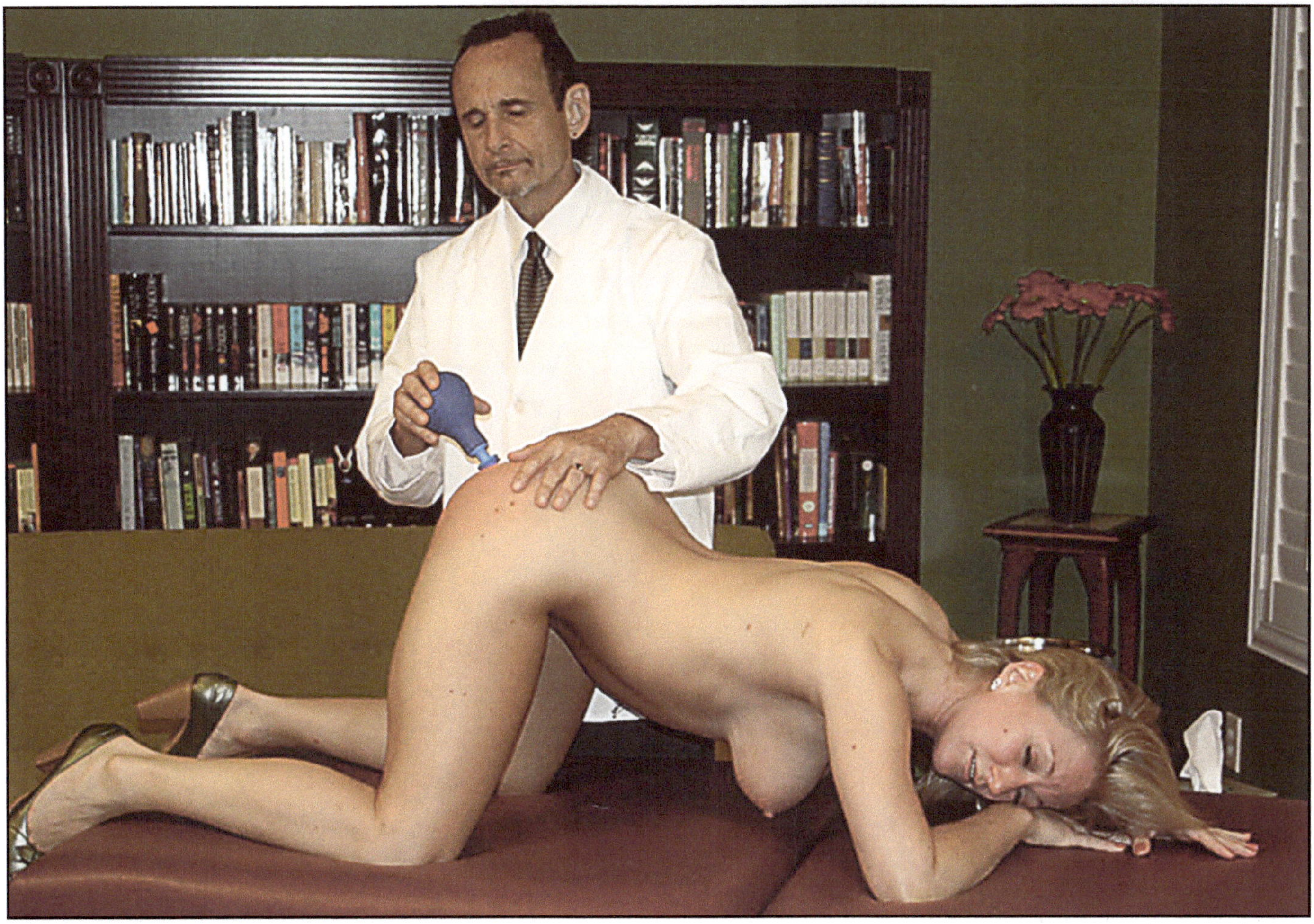

Double Spanking

Strength in Numbers

What dominant male in the world hasn't thought about spanking two beautiful women at the same time? In "Department Store Discipline" Steve Fuller plays a department store manager who must vigorously chastise an errant lead sales girl, (the unflappable but supremely spankable British blonde Amelia Rutherford), and corporally punish a misguided trainee (the lusciously voluptuous brunette Samantha Grace), with an Xmas staff party in between, to insure maximum submissive rowdiness.

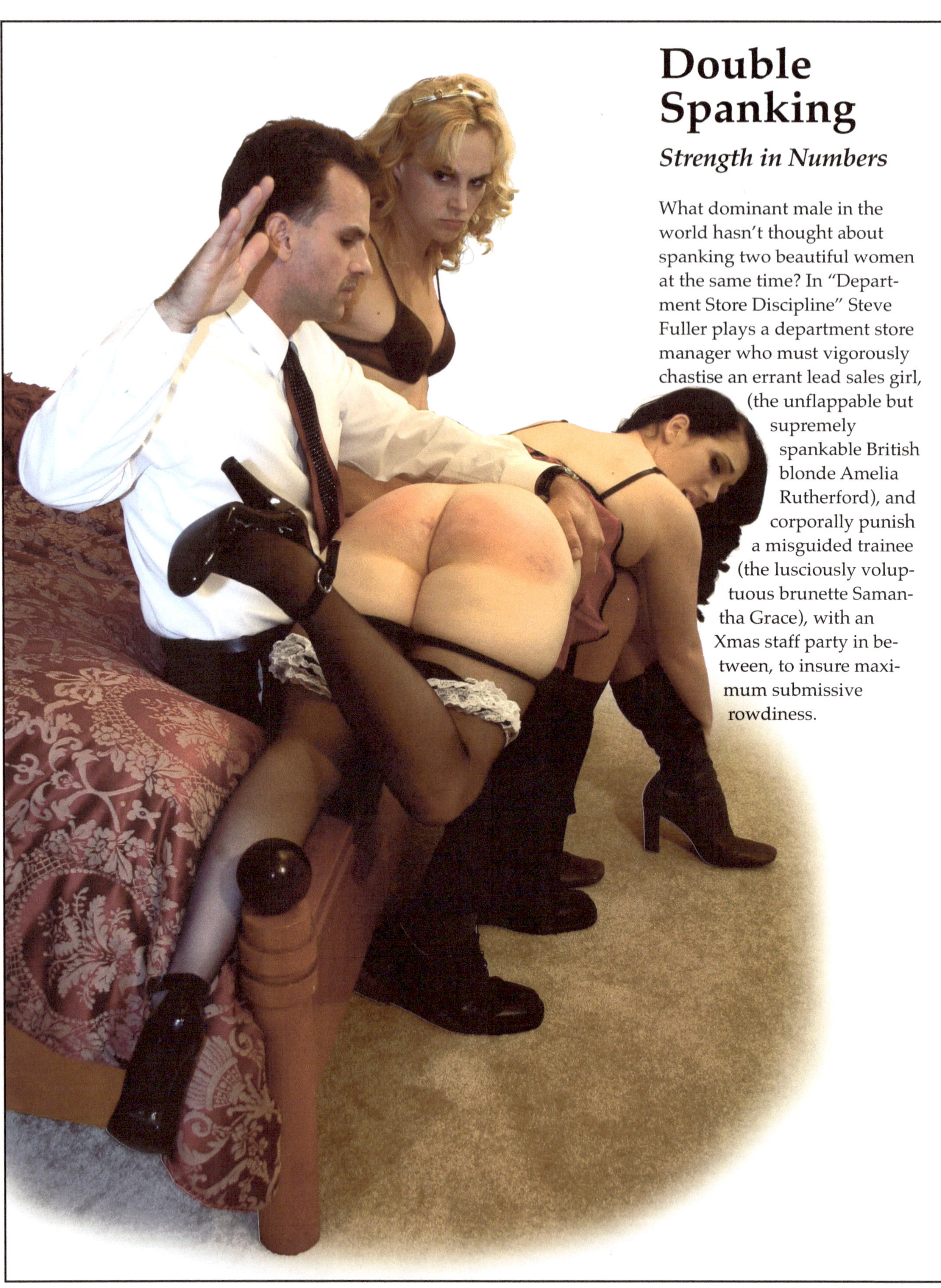

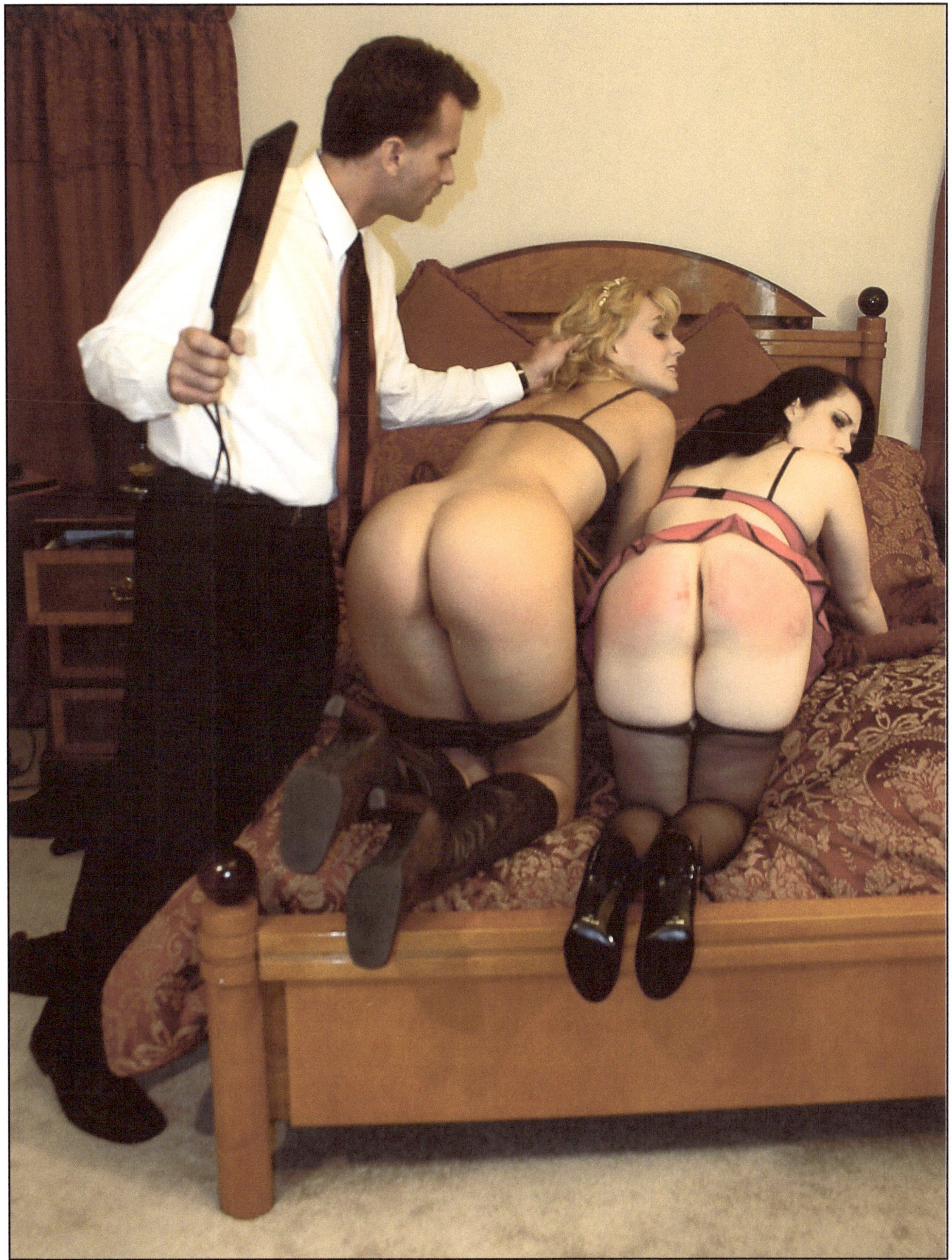

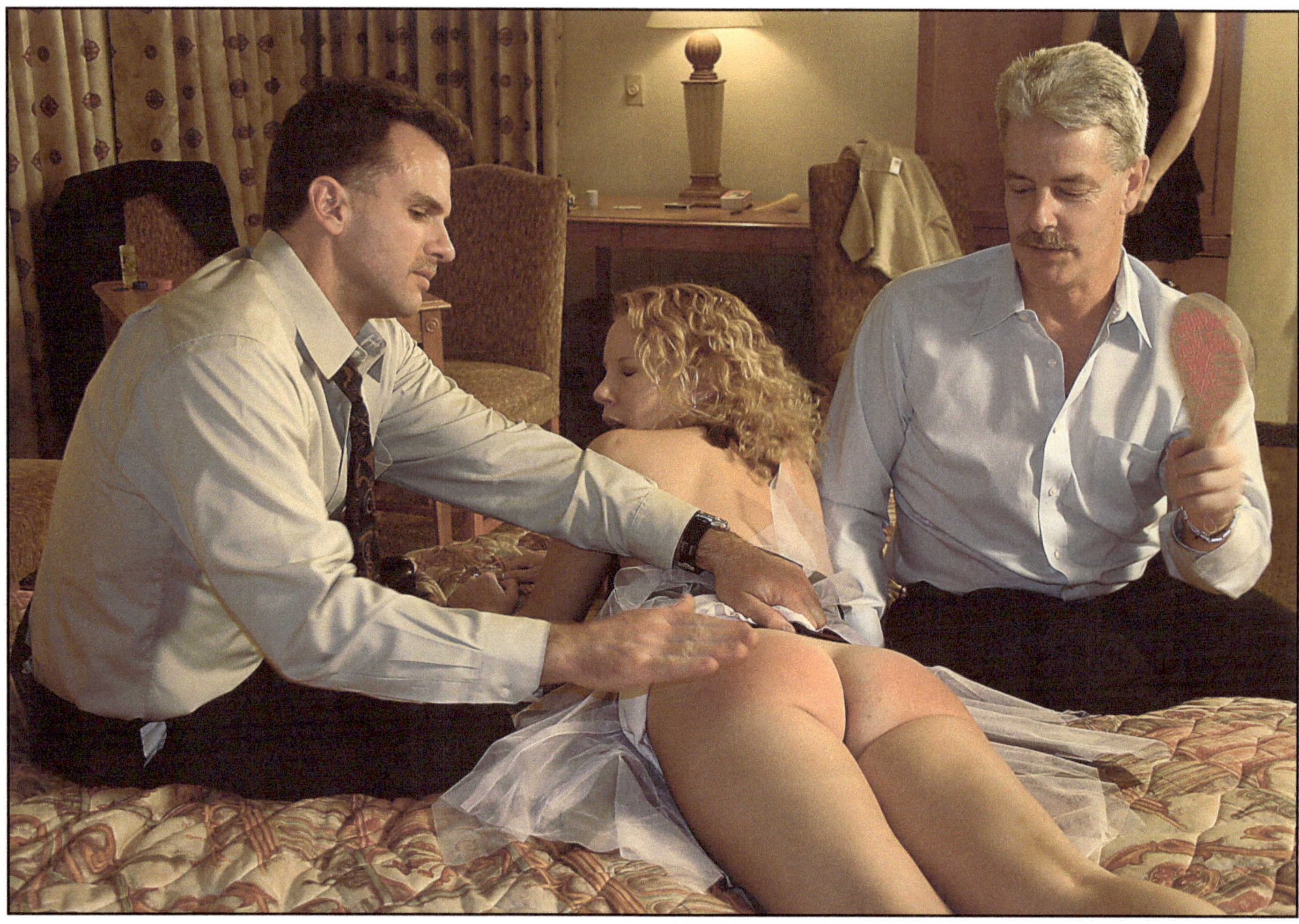

Above
For that matter, what submissive young lady hasn't thought about being spanked by two handsome men at the same time? True spanking enthusiast Amber Pixie Wells plunged deep into this fantasy, enjoying the strict attentions visited upon her by both Steve Fuller and Keith Jones to the hilt in "Cabin Fever".

Opposite
Of course the ultimate spanking fantasy is spanking two girls over the same lap, expertly demonstrated here by the formidable Miss Chris as Headmistress, with lithe, auburn haired Jenni Mack and shapely brunette brat Sarah Gregory portraying the preppie hellions in her charge. This is a maneuver best managed by a tall, powerful woman with strong thighs and a tireless arm and this cheerful and effective Arizona dominant fits that bill beyond compare. When a girl has been spanked by Miss Chris, she feels it for a week.

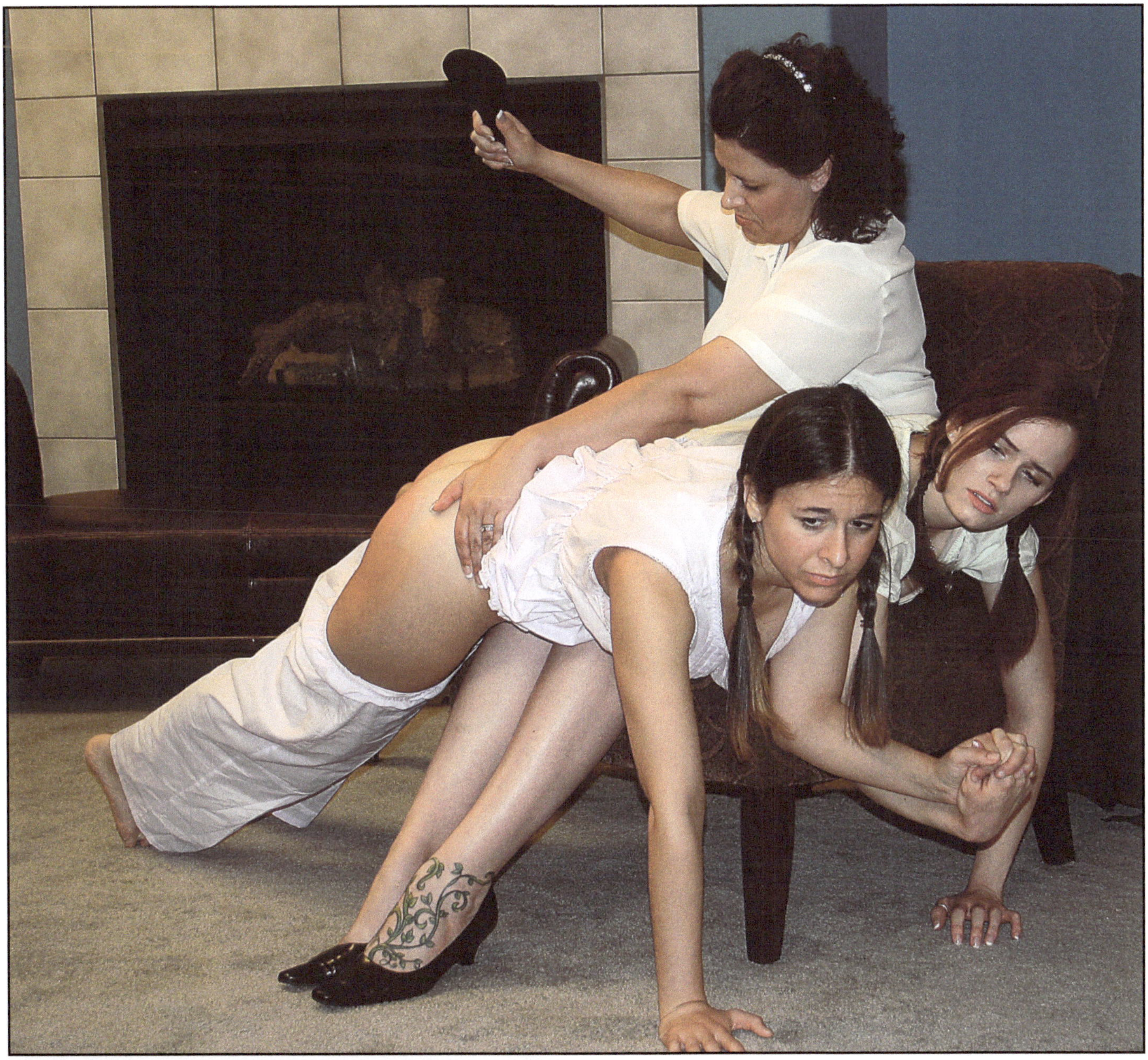

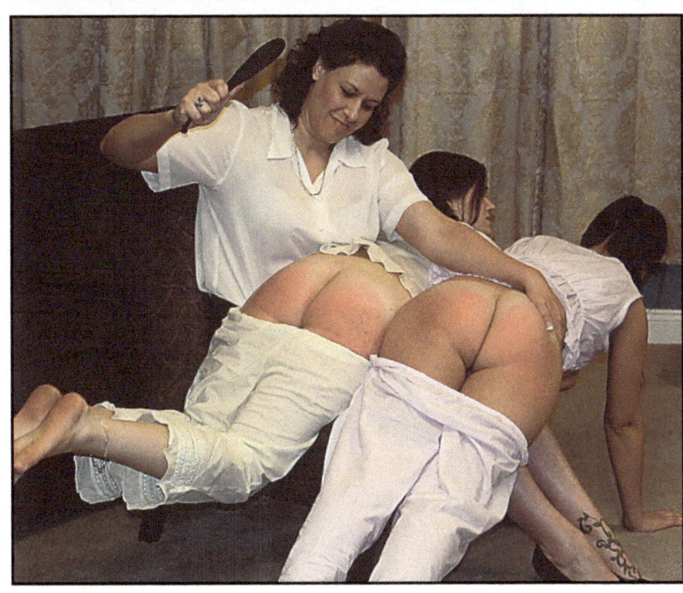

End Pages

Ruffled Rumba Panties

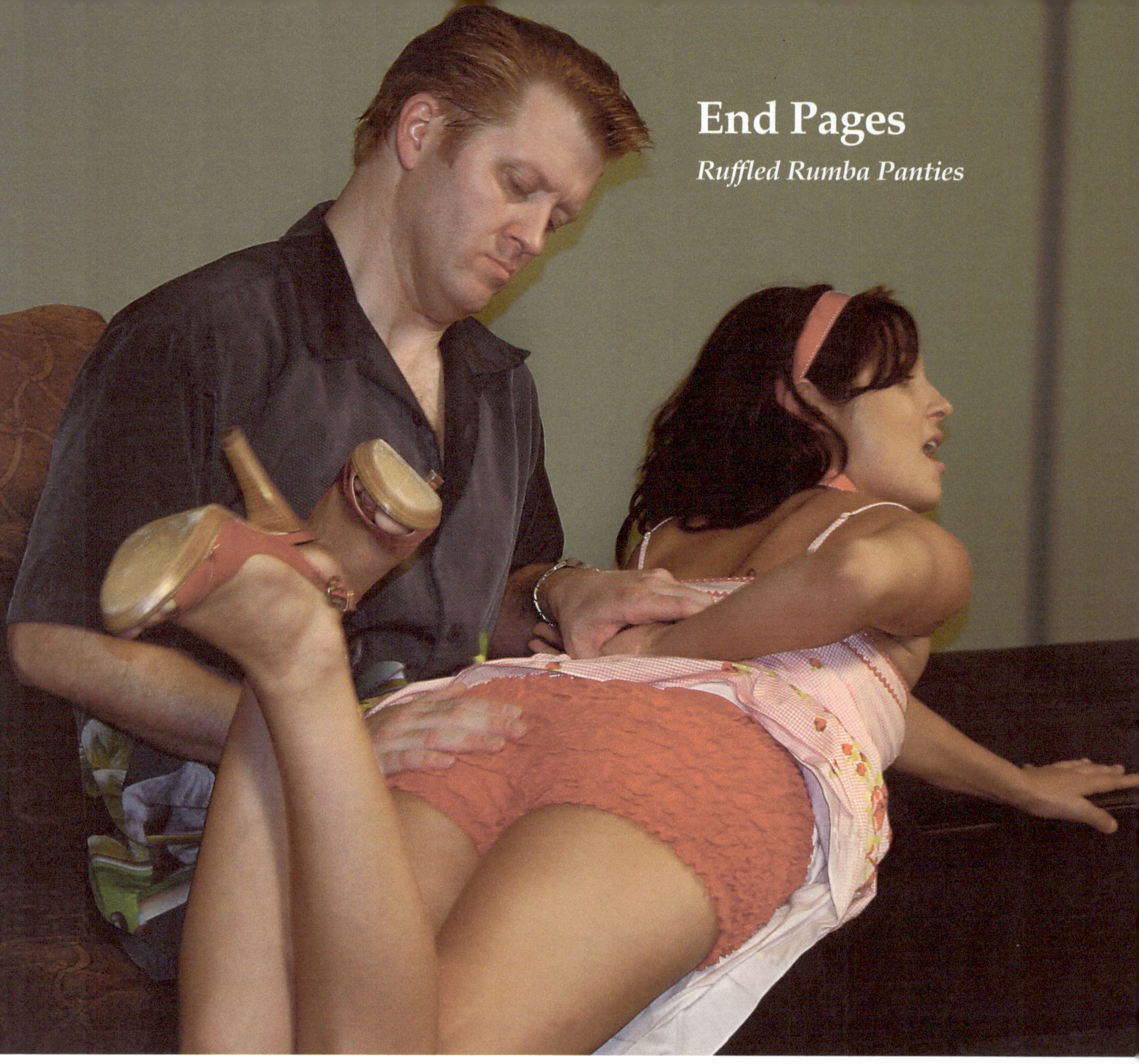

The subject of panties with relation to spanking, could fill an entire book in itself. Most women into spanking couldn't even tell you how many panties they own, because they would be too numerous to count. Real panties, not thongs, are the spankee's most important fashion accessory. And when a girl adorns her stunning bottom in fire engine red ruffled rumba panties, her message is clear: focus your attention here!

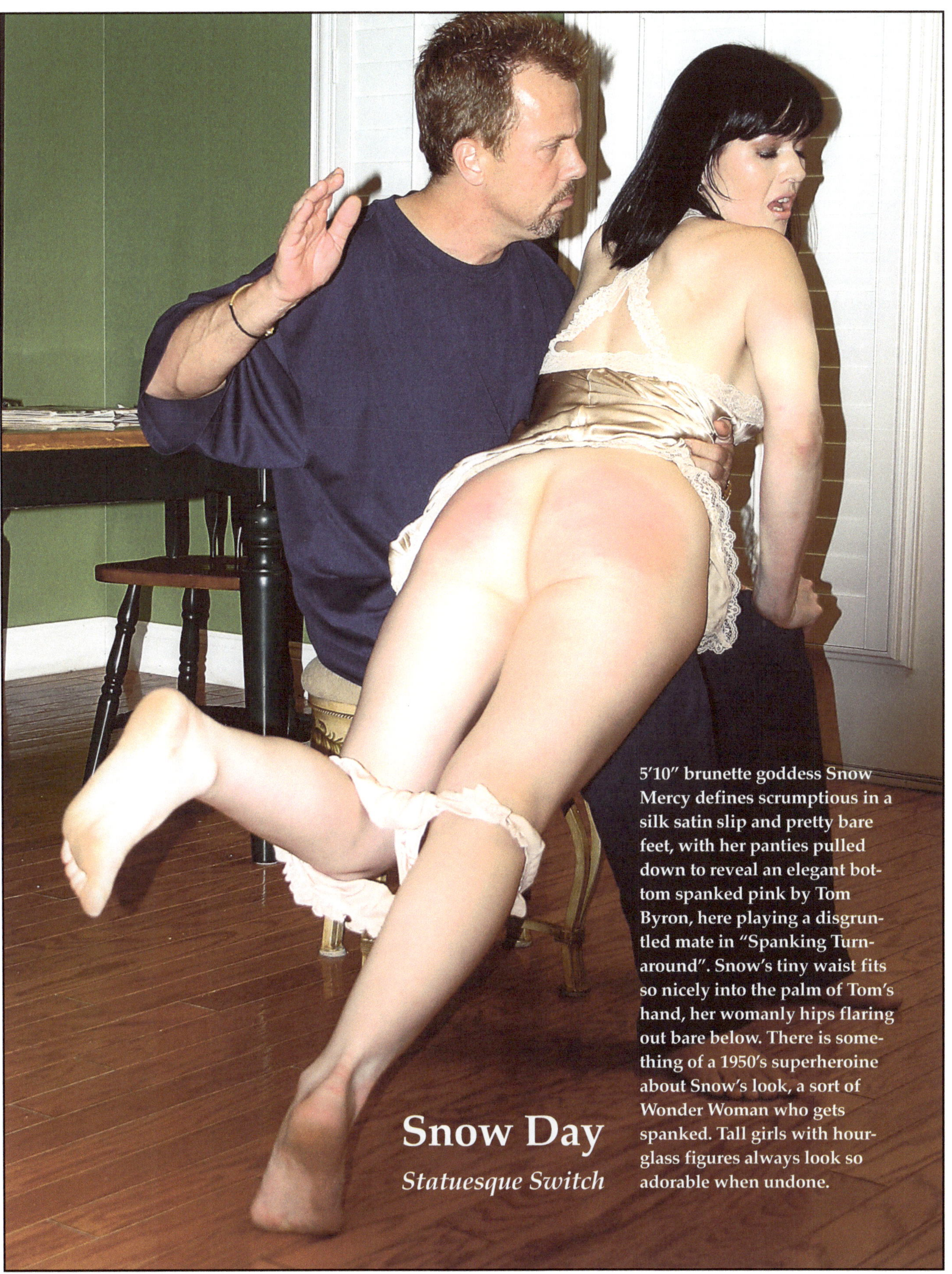

Snow Day

Statuesque Switch

5'10" brunette goddess Snow Mercy defines scrumptious in a silk satin slip and pretty bare feet, with her panties pulled down to reveal an elegant bottom spanked pink by Tom Byron, here playing a disgruntled mate in "Spanking Turnaround". Snow's tiny waist fits so nicely into the palm of Tom's hand, her womanly hips flaring out bare below. There is something of a 1950's superheroine about Snow's look, a sort of Wonder Woman who gets spanked. Tall girls with hourglass figures always look so adorable when undone.

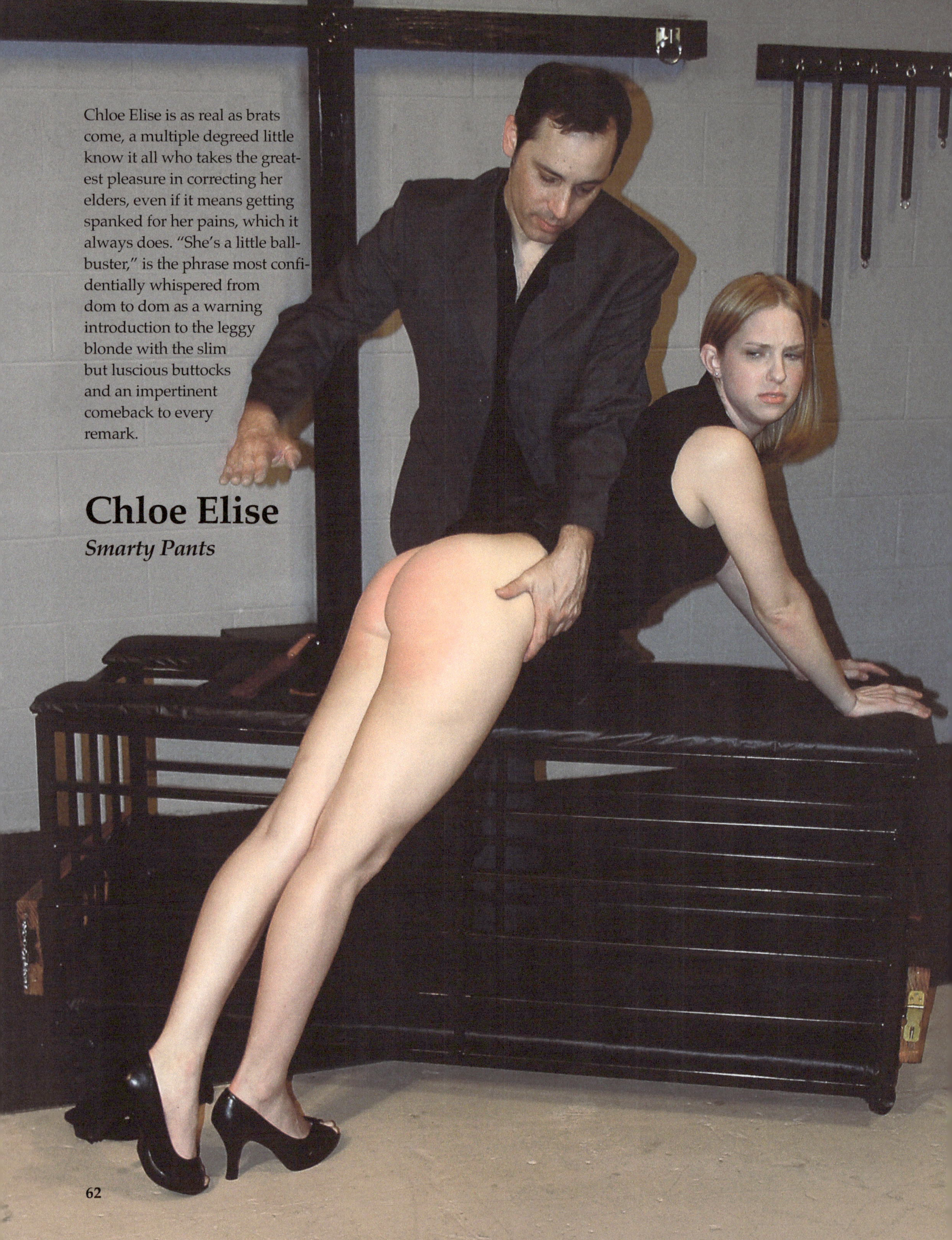

Chloe Elise is as real as brats come, a multiple degreed little know it all who takes the greatest pleasure in correcting her elders, even if it means getting spanked for her pains, which it always does. "She's a little ball-buster," is the phrase most confidentially whispered from dom to dom as a warning introduction to the leggy blonde with the slim but luscious buttocks and an impertinent comeback to every remark.

Chloe Elise

Smarty Pants

Nikki Rouge

Redheaded Firecracker

Lissome Nikki Rouge submits her remarkably beautiful bottom to one of our most traditional spankers, Steve Fuller, in a scene from "Bare Assets" the story of a profligate young woman who must account to her financial advisor for every budgetary misstep, with predictable results, shown here and on our back cover.

In addition to possessing a delightful and vivacious personality, the legs of Cyd Charisse and near perfect proportions, the ballet trained, titian haired Venus has a pain tolerance new scales have to be invented to measure. After three corporal punishment episodes, involving hand, belt and leather strap, Nikki was still well able to withstand a good paddling with the red maple paddle. On which satisfying note we will bring this pleasant sojourn into the Art of Spanking to a happy end.

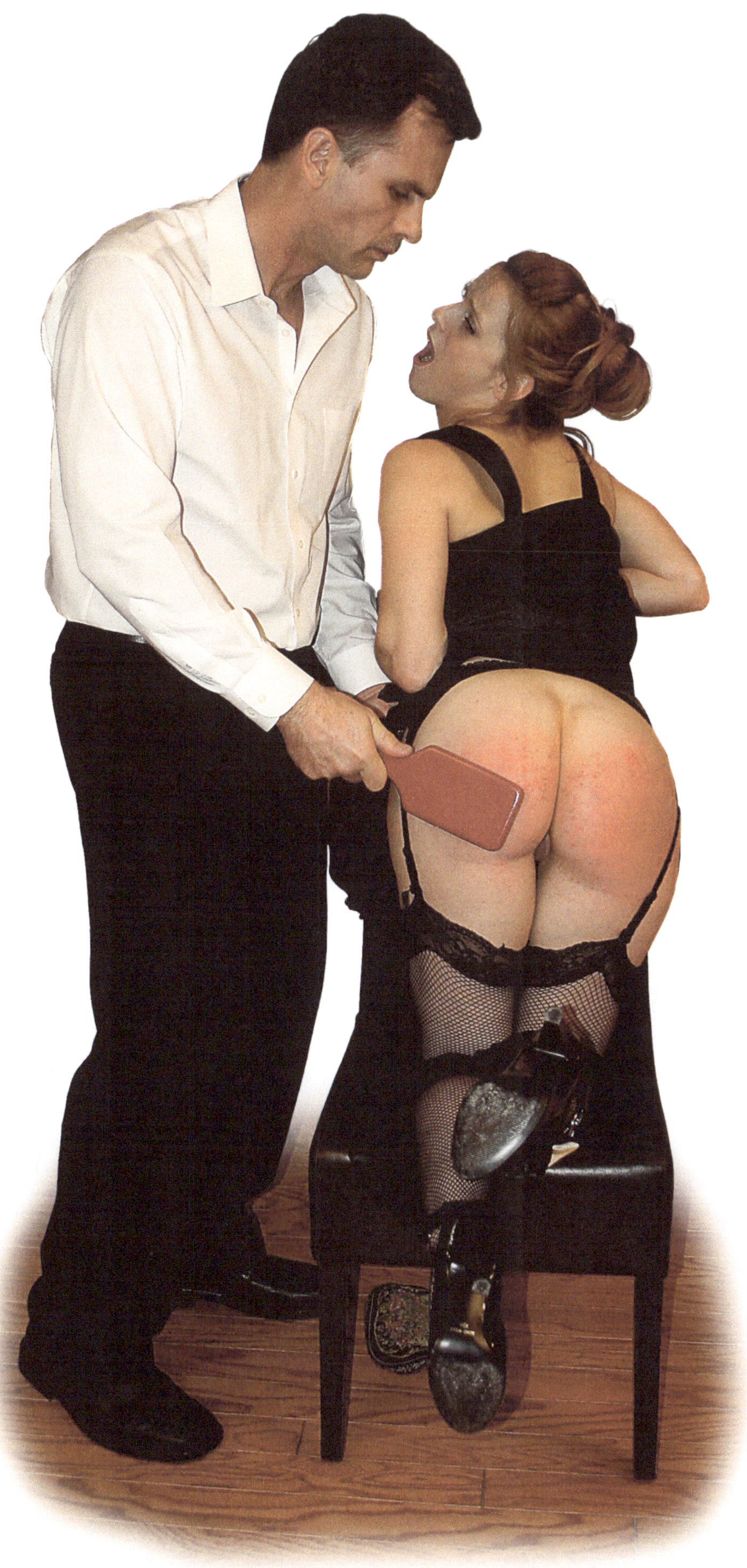

www.ingramcontent.com/pod-product-compliance
Lightning Source LLC
LaVergne TN
LVHW070509120826
845147LV00031BA/349

* 9 7 8 1 9 2 6 9 1 8 0 0 6 *